ATTRACTIVE OPPOSITES

Averil was the kind of woman that Sir Madoc could easily understand and just as easily possess —a ravishing creature who, like her father, a notorious smuggler, believed that nothing should stop her from taking what she wanted, and the only crime was to be caught.

Corralie was a species of female entirely foreign to Madoc—a model of virtue who represented a challenge he could not resist, not to mention a fortune he could not ignore.

Madoc would have liked to have both—but the trouble was, they would not share him.

And as Madoc found his luck running out in a desperate game of international intrigue, he had to choose the lady who would risk all to save him. . . .

THE SMUGGLER'S DAUGHTER

SIGNET REGENCY ROMANCES You'll Enjoy

To order these titles,

please use coupon on

the last page of this book.

THE
SMUGGLER'S
DAUGHTER

Sandra Heath

A SIGNET BOOK
NEW AMERICAN LIBRARY
TIMES MIRROR

Copyright © 1979 by Sandra Heath

SIGNET TRADEMARK REG. U.S. PAT. OFF. AND FOREIGN COUNTRIES
REGISTERED TRADEMARK—MARCA REGISTRADA
HECHO EN CHICAGO, U.S.A.

SIGNET, SIGNET CLASSICS, MENTOR, PLUME AND MERIDIAN BOOKS
are published by The New American Library, Inc.,
1301 Avenue of the Americas, New York, New York 10019

First Printing, August, 1979

1   2   3   4   5   6   7   8   9

PRINTED IN THE UNITED STATES OF AMERICA

1

The sun played leafy shadows over the moss bank beneath the trees, and the clearing was quiet. It was a secret place where only the babbling of the stream and the murmuring of the breeze in the trees broke the silence. The sound of the dogcart came clearly down the unseen lane, and the man turned toward the sycamores that shielded the clearing from the track. Behind him the wooded hillside rose until the bare expanse of Bascombe Heath emerged from the thick skirt of trees; and there, on the top of the heath, the five standing stones shimmered in the heat.

The tawny-haired girl climbed down from the dogcart, fluffing out her yellow muslin skirts before walking toward the man in the dark blue coat and beige breeches.

The air was filled with the scent of early meadowsweet as he smiled at her, and she flushed, overcome with sudden embarrassment. "It was wrong of me to come here like this," she said.

"It was more wrong of me to ask you, Averil."

"It's just—it's just that I've never met anyone like you before," she said.

"But you are engaged to the most eligible nobleman in Dorset," he smiled, reaching out to touch her cheek. The wind ruffled his thick, black hair and she stared at him.

"Lawrence isn't like you, Madoc," she whispered.

"Ah, but he's an infinitely greater catch—a lord, no less." He took her hand and raised it so that the sun flashed on the huge ruby of her ring. "A costly bauble by any standard, and Kendal has fortune enough to keep you in luxury until the end of your days."

"If it wasn't that he bored me so." She looked away. There, it was said. Lawrence bored her so that she could hardly bear to be with him any more.

Madoc raised his eyebrows. "But he loves you, he must do or he would not have asked you to marry him. For a lord to marry Harry Tindling's daughter is surely staggering even in this day and age."

She flushed. "He doesn't know about my father."

"Kendal is a Dorset man and doesn't know that Harry Tindling is Dorset's most notorious smuggler? I don't believe it."

"There are some who don't know. Which makes me wonder—and not for the first time—how *you* know so much, Madoc. You're a stranger in these parts and yet you know about my father. How?"

"By keeping my eyes and ears open at all times. And by paying attention to my aunt's chitter-chatter."

"Lady Agnes? Maybe. And as to your ears and eyes—well, if you have discovered in that way, then it is a great achievement." She studied his dark, handsome face.

"I am a marvel, am I not?" He took her hand

again and raised it to his lips. "You are very beautiful, Averil."

She trembled. "Beauty such as mine takes time and money."

"Beauty is beauty—it must be there in the first place. But your father's money has certainly made a lady of you, a diamond of the first degree."

She drew her hand away, flushing. She'd worked hard to win Lawrence Kendal, and once she'd caught him she'd kept him. But this man, with his wild, black hair and dark, brown eyes, this penniless Welshman, fresh from London where he'd no doubt cut a dash to end all dashes, had entered her life and set her at sixes and sevens with herself. "Why did you come to Dorset, Madoc? Why are you and your sister here now?"

"To stay at Webley Castle with my aunt. Why else? Webley is, after all, mine—as I am the sole male Vaughan since the death of my father and uncle."

"Webley has not seen hide nor hair of you all your life. Lady Agnes has always lived here. Gaming tables, horse races, and fashionable society, that's your life usually. So why come to Chacehampton?"

"Am I on trial, Averil?" he asked softly.

"No," she whispered as he kissed her. "I just want to know about you."

"But why? You see me and I am here." He bent his head and kissed her again.

Corralie urged the horse up the incline of Bascombe Heath toward the standing stones. The sea of Chacehampton Bay was a deep blue where the long wooded promontory of Selney Bill seemed to float. Everything was hazy in the late May sunshine. She reined in by the stones. The Five Warriors. Were they really men turned to stone? She dismounted and took out the hat pin that kept her fashionable beaver hat in place, and her auburn hair tumbled around her shoulders. The on-shore wind was soothing, and she took a long, satisfied breath. This time yesterday she had been bumping and swaying from London in her father's landau; but today London was a lifetime away. Bascombe Heath in the summer was a world of its own. A special, beloved place. And part of everything she most prized.

She watched Lawrence's low racing cutter as it beat steadily west from Chacehampton Bay toward Webley Bay. The elegant two-masted sailing ship dipped and swayed through the choppy water at the end of the outcrop where Webley Castle stood. The *Fair Maid* had never been so close-hauled before, surely he would never get her through those rocks. . . . She held her breath as the cutter's bows swung cleanly through the gap, and then she smiled, remounting Bracken. Down in the tiny, narrow-mouthed bay the *Fair Maid* was turning to run back toward Chacehampton.

Corralie kicked her heel. "Come on, Bracken, we'll be there to meet him." The hooves drummed on the springy ground where young ferns uncurled in the hollows and wild spreads of gorse and heather filled the eye with color. Webley Bay passed from sight as the horse entered Bascombe Woods. The trees were cool and the air damp with the smell of moss. Bracken's hoofbeats were dulled to practically nothing, and the hunter's nervous snorting was the loudest noise in the quiet green glades. Corralie reined in to replace her hat, pushing her disorderly curls beneath it and hoping that she did not present too disreputable a sight when she reached Chacehampton.

Unexpectedly, a jay burst from the bushes ahead, a flash of chattering blue that brought the hunter's head up sharply. Corralie swayed, caught off balance, but as she snatched at the reins the horse was already beyond her control, rearing with his ears flat and his eyes rolling.

"Bracken! *No!*" she screamed as the horse bolted through the dizzy cloak of low branches and leaves, splashing across the stream toward the bank where Averil and Madoc jumped guiltily apart. The blur of trees, sky, and earth was set spinning as the bough of the oak swept Corralie from the saddle and the sweet almond perfume of meadowsweet enveloped her. Before she lost consciousness, she had an uncertain and dreamy impression of two startled faces leaning over her, and then she was floating into the blackness that surrounded her. Beyond that velvet darkness she could still hear Bracken's frightened hoofbeats drumming through the woods.

Averil stared. "It's Corralie Somerford! Do you think she saw us before——?"

"She didn't have time to see anything." Madoc took Corralie's foolish beaver hat and laid it on the grass beside her, and then loosened the tight buttons at the throat of her riding habit. "Reynold Somerford's daughter?"

"Yes. Oh, Madoc, let's get away from here before she comes around. Please!"

"But we can't do that."

"If *she* should realize, Corralie of all people——"

He looked up. "Why 'Corralie of all people'?"

"Because she and Lawrence are close—they grew up together—and if she could break my engagement to him, she would."

"Because you are Harry Tindling's daughter?"

"No. Because she loves Lawrence."

"Money would have married money then, wouldn't it? Somerford's thousands and Kendal's fortune." He looked down at the unconscious girl, gently touching the angry bruise on her forehead.

"Madoc, we can't stay here and wait for her to come around. *Please!*"

"She won't come around for a while yet."

The sound of the Chacehampton church clock carried on the summer breeze. Averil looked in its direction. "It's four o'clock. Lawrence will be coming in soon, and I promised to be there."

He kissed her hand. "Then go to him," he said softly.

"What about——?"

"I will take her to Webley Castle and my lady aunt's ministrations."

"Shall I see you again?" She blushed at having asked.

"Of course."

She glanced briefly at Corralie and then picked up her reticule, going to where the pony and dog-cart were hidden by the sycamores.

Madoc watched her, his face expressionless. Pray God this would not get out of hand, for the last thing he wanted was for her to break her engagement with Kendal. If it were not for the fact that she was so important to——

Corralie stirred, her lips moving. Madoc brought his horse and then crouched down beside her again. She was so beautiful. And wealthy. And in love with a milksop like Lawrence Kendal. He smiled. The winning of Corralie Somerford would be no contest at all with only Kendal to run against.

As he picked her up he trapped some meadowsweet and the perfume drifted over them both. Pollen fell on the dark red velvet, specks of golden dust on the costly cloth. Her head lolled against his shoulder, her hair dragging through the cream-colored flowers as he carried her to the horse.

"Steady Beau, steady now with so precious a cargo," he murmured as he lifted her onto the saddle, mounting carefully behind her and easing her back into his arms once more. Her lips were parted slightly as if she were about to kiss some lover. Madoc saw no reason not to give in to temptation, and he bent his head to kiss her.

She moved in his arms. "Lawrence?"

So Averil was right, Corralie Somerford *did* want Kendal for herself.

She drifted on the brink of consciousness. "Lawrence?" she murmured again.

"Yes?" He was curious to see what else she might do, but her body went limp again.

He kicked his heel and The Beau moved away, splashing across the stream and cantering easily along the narrow lane toward Webley Castle. Madoc whistled lightly to himself. For everyone's sake, he hoped that Corralie would not recall what she had come upon. He looked down at her again. What man in his right senses would choose Averil Tindling before Corralie Somerford?

2

Seagulls screamed over the low cliff beyond the castle gardens and Madoc closed the rusty window to shut out their noise. Corralie lay on the ornate four-poster bed and Madoc's old aunt fussed anxiously at the bedside.

"You've been sure to send for Doctor Yattere now, Madoc?"

"Yes."

"Oh dear, and today was meant to be such an auspicious day."

"Auspicious?" Madoc raised an eyebrow.

"Why yes. It's Urban's Day—always an auspicious day."

"For vintners, maybe. Beyond that it is merely the twenty-fifth of May in the year eighteen hundred and fourteen."

She sniffed and patted her mobcap. "As I said—an auspicious day. Were I to take my conclusions further, I would add up the number of letters in Corralie's name, the number in your name, and the number of the day of the month. That would give me absolute confidence. You'll find for certain that the resultant number is even, which means she will recover very well."

Madoc looked out of the window for a moment and then smiled. "The resultant number happens to be twenty-three, *ma tante*."

She ignored him and leaned forward to put a cool, damp cloth to Corralie's forehead. "Oh dear, whatever will Reynold say!"

"It's Reynold, is it? And how long have you been on first-name terms with Dorset's richest man?"

"Long enough. *Dieu*, Madoc, I've lived here for twenty years now, how should I *not* know Corralie and her father? We move in the same circles."

"And share the same hare-brained notions about stars, planets, herbs, and numbers! A pair of redoubtable eccentrics! But you neglected to tell me that the other half of this act was possessed of so beautiful a daughter."

Lady Agnes sat back and looked at him. "Nor would I! You may be my nephew, Madoc, but you are also a villainous scoundrel with too much of an eye to your own gain. Apart from that, I happen to like Corralie."

"The Lord protect me from guardian angels," he said with mock feeling.

She smiled across the room at him. "And the Lord also protect sweet creatures like Corralie here from wolves like you."

"Herb witch!"

Lady Agnes squeezed the cloth in the bowl of cool water again and then put it once more to the girl's forehead. "How much longer is that mischievous physician going to be? I swear I'll give him a good wigging when he comes! It's over an hour since we sent word down to Chacehampton. And there's been no word from Reynold either, now that I think of it. Oh no, now I remember, he's gone to Dorchester today."

"Ah, so you are *au fait* with his every appointment, are you?"

"He asked me to accompany him, but I declined. I do not like journeying in that cursed landau of his—it sways from side to side as if it were at sea."

"Even on this *auspicious* day?"

She threw him a glance and refrained from answering.

He sat in a chair and crossed his legs elegantly before him, looking at Corralie. "I tell you, *ma tante,* for once I actually pray that your belief in portents and so on is well justified."

"She'll not be won with a crooking of *your* little finger, Madoc—however handsome, accomplished, and fashionable that exquisite finger may be."

"Can you not consider just for once," he said with injured eyes fixed upon her, "that maybe beneath this veneer I am lovable and sweet——?"

"No, I cannot. You've reached the age of thirty-three without convincing me that you are anything but an adventurer. A charming one, but nonetheless an adventurer. You have also reached this age without ever visiting me here—oh, you come to my London home when I am there, but as to putting yourself to visit your poor old aunt down here in the back of nowhere, that's another matter. Why *have* you come? And with Catti, too? I am so taken aback it's taken me these past two months to recover."

"What a waspish tongue you have! I am scarce surprised that my late uncle made a somewhat early exit from this life! He did it to preserve his sanity."

The old lady smiled fondly at him. "It was Trafalgar that put an end to him, not my tongue! *Diawch,* but you're a Vaughan through and through, Madoc. Scoundrels, all of them. Except Catti."

"But lovable?"

"Perhaps. Where's Catti now?"

"Mooning."

Lady Agnes tutted. "It's almost unhealthy, do you know that? Sitting there gazing at that man's portrait for hour after hour."

"That *man* is her husband."

"He's also—— Oh, listen, isn't that Doctor Yattere's horse now? He always rides that creature as if he's got a week to go a mile. Trit-trot, trit-trot—I doubt that the old nag knows how to go faster after all these years. I'll go and meet him."

"Well, don't confound him with numbers and magic, will you?"

He heard her laugh as she went down the stone steps leading toward the walled courtyard of the old fortified manor house.

Corralie stirred on the bed and her eyes opened.

"Miss Somerford?"

She turned to look up at him. Her eyes were very green. "Who are you?"

"Sir Madoc Vaughan, at your service." He bowed his head.

"Vaughan? You are Lady Agnes's——?"

"Nephew."

She closed her eyes at the pain in her head. "What happened? Why am I here?"

He studied her. "You—don't remember anything?"

"No. At least, I remember being up by the Five Warriors. I was going to meet Lawrence at Chacehampton. I *think* I was, anyway."

He glanced away to hide the ghost of a smile which he knew was on his face at the thought of both Averil and Corralie waiting on the quayside to greet Lawrence Kendal.

She watched his thin profile, taking in his dark blue coat and nankin breeches. There was something vaguely familiar about him, and she felt sure that she must have seen him before. "Are you sure we have not met before, Sir Madoc?"

"I am certain, Miss Somerford, that had we met before I would most definitely have remembered."

"In London, perhaps? I was there until the day before yesterday."

"I assure you, we have not met before."

They heard voices on the steps and then Lady Agnes's mulberry silk skirts rustled as she entered the room with Dr. Yattere.

"Ah, Corralie, you are back in the conscious world! I did not think that we would meet again after all these months in such odd circumstances. How are you feeling?"

"I ache everywhere, Lady Agnes."

Dr. Yattere put down his bag. "And you will for some time to come, Miss Corralie. Now then, let's have a look at you."

He examined her carefully, frowning and shaking his head as he inspected the bruise on her temple. "I don't like the look of *that*, young lady. Out on that damned brute of a horse again, were you? If I've warned you once, I've warned you countless times not to ride it. Lord Kendal must have been tipsy the day he purchased it for you."

"Bracken is a good horse. Oh, Sir Madoc—was my horse all right?"

"Perfectly—as he passed me, but I thought it more pressing to attend to you than to pursue your nag."

She smiled. "He will have gone home—he always does."

Madoc raised his eyebrows. "The beast has done this before?"

Dr. Yattere interrupted quickly. "Yes, it has! I

will have a word with your father this time, Miss Corralie. I've been attending you since the day you were brought into this world, and I consider myself to be your friend as well as your physician, and I tell you this—if you continue riding that sway-backed monstrosity, I'll be attending you on the day you leave this world as well!"

"Bracken's not sway-backed!"

He closed his bag with a snap. "I cannot imagine what possessed Kendal to buy it for you!"

"He bought it because I so admired it."

The doctor smiled fondly at her. "Aye, well, you could always wind him around your finger, could you not?" He cleared his throat embarrassedly. "At least——"

"At one time perhaps I could," she said with a little smile, turning her head away.

The doctor bent to examine the bruise again. "I am not at all happy about this. Lady Agnes, I would feel a great deal easier in my mind if I knew she was not to be moved for a day or so."

"But of course, doctor, she must remain here at Webley. No, Corralie, I will hear no more argument. You must of course be my guest. Besides, Catti will be delighted to have your company, for she is a little lonely."

Corralie looked at the doctor. "If you are sure?"

"I *am* sure—I must know if that contusion is simply that and nothing more serious. Now Lady Agnes, I will leave this laudanum to take away the pain she undoubtedly feels. A low dosage, if you please." He cleared his throat again. "And—er—no herbal remedies of which I know nothing."

The old lady bridled. "My dear doctor, are there any herbal remedies about which you know *any-thing*?"

"I believe we will have this argument until doomsday, my lady. Just take good care of her."

"With laudanum? Tincture of opium? A herbal remedy if I ever heard of one—and one which *I* would hesitate to use. *Ever.*"

"Yes. Well, I will take my leave of you." He tapped his hat onto his head and looked down at Corralie again. "And I *will* be speaking with your father about that animal. *And* with Lord Kendal, should I happen across him."

Corralie closed her eyes and nodded. "As you wish, Doctor Yattere. And thank you for coming."

"I will come again in a day or so, and then if I am satisfied all is well, then you may go home. Good day to you, Lady Agnes. Sir Madoc."

Madoc bowed and went to show the doctor out, leaving his aunt with Corralie. The old lady snorted angrily.

"What a ramshackle fellow he is—his very looks would damn him!"

"You and he will never see eye to eye, Lady Agnes."

"To be sure. Now then, I will prepare some dandelion tonic for you——oh, it's no trouble, no trouble at all. Dandelion is ruled by Jupiter, don't you know, and is therefore soothing, cheering, and benevolent. It cannot *help* but be good for you. And I have some good green hyssop to put on that bruise on your forehead. Oh, my poor Corralie, how dreadful for you to take such a fall on your first full day back with us."

"Doctor Yattere was right, it was my own fault for riding Bracken."

"It must be the first time that man's ever been right about anything. And how did you like London?"

"Very much. But I danced at Almack's as if I was possessed of two left feet—I trod on Sir Jeremy Thamesdon's new patent slippers and made him rather cross with me."

"Everything makes that dandified fop cross. It's his trademark, don't you know?"

"No, I didn't."

"Well, we've talked enough. I will bring the tea and dress the wound."

"And the laudanum?"

Lady Vaughan looked at the little phial on the table. "A little, perhaps."

"I *do* ache a great deal."

Lady Vaughan picked up the phial and bustled from the room. Corralie closed her eyes. If she could only *remember* the accident—— But it all was an impenetrable wall of forgetfulness.

3

Madoc paused with his hand on Corralie's door. Slow footsteps were descending the tower steps at the end of the passageway. He watched the old door open.

"Catti? I was just seeing if our guest is all right."

The girl smiled at him. She was small and pale, with golden hair piled expertly at the back of her head in a tumble of Grecian curls. Her eyes were large and dark and he saw immediately that she had been crying.

"Tears again, *cariad?*" He left the door and crossed the passageway to his sister, putting his arm around her thin shoulders and squeezing her gently.

"Oh, Madoc, I cannot help it. I miss him so."

Madoc glanced at the closed door and then steered her away to stand by the narrow slit window which looked out over the sloping gardens toward the sea. They could hear the waves breaking on the pebbles of Webley Bay, and the freshness of salt air drifted through the open window.

"It's not for so much longer now, Catti."

"But it's so dangerous." Catti's hands twisted her

handkerchief until it was an unrecognizable rag. "For you both."

He kissed the top of her head. "You are without your mobcap again—Aunt Agnes will have something to say about such a lack of propriety."

"Poor Aunt Agnes. It's not right what we do, is it?" She looked up at him.

"There is no other way, *cariad*. But we cannot tell her, can we? Mm?" He stared out at the deep blue sea.

She felt his arm suddenly tighten and his body stiffen. "What is it?"

"Out there. Look. A damned naval sloop!"

They watched the three-masted warship running before the breeze, her sails white and her low, sleek body cutting easily through the waves. Madoc leaned through the window to look eastward toward Chacehampton Bay. "The pilot cutter. Oh, sweet Lord, Catti, I think the navy is coming to Chacehampton!"

Catti's eyes widened as she stared up at her brother. "But Madoc—you must be mistaken."

"I am not. The cutter's signaling now. Now what in God's name does that sloop have to come sniffing around for? I'll find out, somehow or other. I've got to, haven't I?" He smiled at her reassuringly, tapping the end of her nose with his fingertip. "Don't worry—it's probably nothing."

"And if it's not?"

"We'll cross that one when we come to it."

The sloop and the pilot cutter had passed from view now, and Catti straightened her crumpled handkerchief. "And how did you proceed with Tindling's daughter?"

"So personal a question?" he teased.

"Answer it, then."

"I proceeded well enough."

"That I'd warrant, my handsome brother." She smiled.

"It's the one thing I'm master of."

"Did you find out?"

"Give me time, sweetheart, give me time. These things cannot be rushed."

"But we *have* to know!"

"I think I shall have to request Aunt Agnes to infuse some damned herbal tea or other to calm you down, Catti. There is time enough to find out what is necessary."

"There isn't. This was delivered today when you were otherwise occupied in Bascombe Woods." She took a folded note from her reticule.

"Who brought it?"

"The same man as before. See the date? He's brought it forward a month. Full moon night in May, it says. That's tomorrow night, Madoc."

He nodded. "Well, Tindling's safe enough—I nosed around this morning and heard a whisper that the *Laura* is still being refitted somewhere. But Kendal's another matter. And now that thrice-cursed sloop!"

"Lord Kendal is no problem, surely?"

"Yes, he is——he's taken to night sailing. I've been watching. Over the last few days or so he's been out and maneuvering here, there, and everywhere in the bay. Well, I can have him attended to, but not the sloop—that's a little too risky, eh, *cariad?*"

"She looked well armed."

"Eighteen six-pounders."

"And the *Belle Marie?*"

"Armed, but not so well. I'll go in to Chacehampton tomorrow and find out what I can." He kissed Catti's pale cheek. "It will be all right, now, do you hear me?"

She hugged him. "How is our guest?"

"Beautiful and rich."

"That's *not* what I meant." She looked up at him. "So that's why you brought her here, is it? You've always been looking for a suitable heiress, and now you think you've found her?"

"What is there to lose?"

"Nothing, I suppose."

"There is a slight problem. She came upon my idyllic meeting with *la Tindling*. As yet, however, she doesn't remember anything."

"Aunt Agnes says that she and Lord Kendal were once very close."

"So I believe. Pray for me tonight, Catti—pray that my heiress doesn't recall anything about today. Let Kendal have his smuggler's daughter. And let me have Miss Corralie Somerford."

"You seem very sure that you will win her. I hope she gives you a good run for your money, Madoc Vaughan, for you are becoming unbearably conceited."

"Don't you want your only brother to be happily married?"

"*I* married for love—*you* it would seem, are set only upon marrying for money."

"A base lie!"

They smiled at each other.

"Come on down now," he said, "and we'll have a glass or two of something stronger than dandelion tea, eh?"

She looked out over the empty sea again. The sun was setting in the west, tipping the waves with crimson and spreading gold, red, and orange rays across the clear turquoise sky.

"Tomorrow night," she whispered. "I can scarce believe it——"

At Corralie's door, Madoc looked in. She lay in the immense bed, her eyes closed and her rich auburn hair half hiding her face.

Catti looked at her. "She *is* beautiful, Madoc."

"Won't we make a handsome couple?" he said with a grin. His sister dug him in the ribs and they went down the steps toward the great hall of the fortified manor house.

The butler was throwing open the double oak doors leading to the courtyard and they saw a landau swinging beneath the gatehouse, its black lacquerwork shining and its flickering oil lamps throwing weak lights in the gathering darkness. Flies and moths congregated around those lights as the landau lurched to a standstill, its six well-matched grays sweating and stamping. The footman jumped down from his perch to lower the steps by the coach's door.

"My future father-in-law, I do believe," whispered Madoc as Reynold Somerford climbed down from the landau.

He stood on the cobbles, opening a tiny snuff box and delicately taking a pinch as he gazed around. He was dressed in the fashion of thirty years earlier, with a freshly powdered periwig and a bright blue satin coat that was full and low-waisted. His brightly colored waistcoat was also low and he wore breeches and garters, and his high-heeled shoes had large golden buckles. Reynold Somerford did not approve of the modern, revealing fashions adopted by gentlemen—— His sharp little eyes moved disapprovingly over Madoc's tight-fitting trousers and hessians. *Nothing left to the imagination!*

"Good evening to you, Madoc. Lady Catherine."

Catti bobbed a little curtsey and smiled at him. "We began to think you would not get here tonight, Mister Somerford."

"Damned business in Dorchester took longer than I thought. How is she? I received word only that she fell from that dratted beast."

Madoc nodded. "She is asleep at the moment.

Doctor Yattere thinks it best that she stay here for a day or so."

"Does he, be damned? Well, the fellow's a good man—if a trifle conventional. Can I see my daughter?"

"But of course, of course. Please come in. Catti, go and tell Aunt Agnes that Mister Somerford is here. If you will follow me, sir."

Reynold looked down at his daughter's still figure. "Curse that damned four-legged demon. Well, it's the last time she'll ride it—Kendal can have the beggar back again! I should have sent it back to him when she was in London, but I couldn't bring myself to upset her. Bracken! I'd as soon call it Tickweed."

"I would have imagined Lord Kendal to be an excellent judge of horses," said Madoc.

"Maybe. But he can't judge women, and that's an indisputable fact." Reynold bent with difficulty to kiss Corralie's face, pushing back the thick hair. "Got her mother's looks, don't you know. Aye, it's Georgiana I see in Corry."

"Your daughter is very beautiful, Mister Somerford."

"Came as a surprise to you, did it? Eh? An old bear like me with such an angel for a child?"

"Yes, it did," said Madoc with a faint smile.

Reynold grinned suddenly. "I suppose I rather asked for that, didn't I? Now then, you're sure she's all right? I mean—I'd get the Regent's own doctors if I thought she needed them."

"Yattere seemed only concerned over the bruise on her forehead."

"Beneath all that damned hyssop?"

"Yes."

"Jupiter weed—your aunt thinks she knows everything, but *I* know it should be a Venus herb.

Root of wymote, *that's* what should be dressing that poor bruise right now. She don't hold with that plant though, your aunt—some fool notion she's got in her head. Begging your pardon, of course."

"Don't beg *my* pardon, Mister Somerford, for I don't hold with *any* of it."

"Reynold. The name's Reynold. I've known your aunt for so long now, and you've been here for about two months. Damn it, you can't go on calling me Mister Somerford, it's so formal."

"Then Reynold it is." Madoc bowed. "Shall we go down now, and leave your daughter to sleep in peace?"

"Indeed so, indeed so."

They descended the stone steps where each landing had an attendant suit of armor and where the walls were hung with brightly stitched tapestries. "Well, Madoc, and what crack-brained notion brought you and your sister down here to the wilds of Dorset, eh? London's your stamping ground."

"Catti's health is not good and we thought the sea air would benefit her."

"Foreign Office, aren't you?"

"I was."

"Past tense, eh?"

"In a manner of speaking."

Reynold surveyed the younger man thoughtfully. "Trod on sensitive toes, I gather."

"You would seem to be well informed."

"Just because I never stir from Dorset, it don't mean that I'm a country bumpkin, Madoc. Ah well, you'll live without the Foreign Office, no doubt."

"No doubt." Madoc opened the ancient doors of the great hall and stood aside for Reynold to go inside.

Lady Agnes set her heavy book down and took

off her spectacles. "Ah, Reynold, how pleased I am
to see you." She held out her hand, smiling.

"Agnes. In your element, eh? Dosing and infus-
ing poor Corralie."

"And you don't approve, I take it?"

"Hyssop!" His nose twitched.

"Not that drivel about wymote again!" she
snapped, bristling immediately. "I would have
thought by now that you would have seen a small
glimpse of daylight through that mist of idiocy!"

Catti stared and Madoc rolled his eyes. "Aunt
Agnes! That is hardly polite behavior——"

"Don't interrupt me, Madoc."

"Hobbyhorses can be excessively boring, Agnes,"
retaliated Reynold, sitting down and straightening
his periwig. "*Excessively* so."

"It says here in this herbal——" She bent to sweep
up the ancient book she had been reading. "There,
right *there!*"

He peered at it. "Damn it, Agnes, it's in Welsh!
You are on safe ground there, for I cannot argue
one way or the other, can I? You might as well
write it in Russian!"

She grinned at him. "Well, the hyssop is there
now, and doing its work brilliantly."

"If you say so," he said resignedly.

She positively beamed at his capitulation.
"Besides, Venus is not in good aspect now——
wymote is therefore *out!*"

"If you say so."

"Don't keep saying that."

"Great heavens, Agnes, I cannot win either way.
If I argue, it's not right, and if I give in, that's not
right either."

Madoc poured some Madeira and looked at the
two on either end of the sofa. "I cannot understand
how two intelligent, normally sane persons can be
so unreasonable over damned leaves."

Reynold peered at him. "Oh, foolish boy, statements like that can cause a veritable battlefield to materialize in this hall. Let us turn to safer topics. If Corry's to stay here a day or so, should I have her maid and so on sent over? I mean, I have little notion of what clothes she'll need."

Catti smiled. "There's no need, sir, for your daughter is quite welcome to share my clothes, toiletries, *and* the services of my maid."

"That's most generous of you, Lady Catherine, most generous indeed."

"It's not. I'm just pleased she's here, for I have missed—company."

Reynold sipped the Madeira. "Not added anything to this, have you, Agnes?"

"Such as?"

"I don't know—I *do* know you fancy yourself at blending."

"Arsenic would seem a capital notion right now, Reynold Somerford," she said tartly. "Now drink up and stop being so obstinate."

He smiled fondly at her. "Agnes, if I didn't come here for the occasional argument, I doubt that I'd survive another winter—you are a positive tonic. Your health."

Madoc sat down. "I see there's a navy ship in Chacehampton Bay, Reynold."

"Yes, so I noticed as I drove over. D'you know, Agnes, I rather fancied it was the *Janus*."

She blinked. "Should that mean anything to me?"

"I thought you might remember old Chadders."

"Captain Chadwick? But of course—the *Janus* is his ship?"

"If it is the *Janus*. It was the same class of sloop. I tried to get a good look at the figurehead, but she was anchored too far out in the bay, right in the lee of Selney Bill. By God, it's a good few years since the navy honored Chacehampton, eh? There'll be a deal of panic until everyone realizes there's not to be a press." Reynold looked at Madoc. "Chadwick and I were at school together—he's a bit stuffy, but he'll do."

"One wonders why the sloop is here at all." Madoc glanced at Catti.

"Does one? Oh, yes, I suppose one does. Could be anything, of course. To be honest, I suspect it's because Harry Tindling's cutter sank that Revenue ship a month ago. Damn fool, he should have known they couldn't let him get away with that. But this is between you, me, and Hobby's cat, you understand."

"Tindling's a shrewd customer."

Reynold shrugged. "So I thought——but he knew the *Laura* could outrun anything the Revenue men have got, so why did he stop to fight? Eh? He ended up with the *Laura* damaged, one less government cutter, and a good deal of odium. The Revenuers hadn't even got him cornered."

Lady Agnes looked at him. "But still you took your cask of cognac from that particular shipment, Reynold. Shame on you."

"You're right—I sit here pronouncing my disapproval, but still I take what's going. Most shameful. Do you know, Madoc—most folk around these parts know that the *Laura* is Tindling's, and they know who her crew are—but still the Revenuers can't pinpoint *any* sort of proof to get him into gaol. Makes you think, eh?"

"Too many influential people have fingers in the pie, Reynold," said Madoc quietly.

"Aye, we do, don't we?" Reynold raised his glass. "But then, that's what it's all about, ain't it? Well, I must be getting back now—I'm sore all over from journeying today, and my cool bed calls me. Thank you again for all you're doing for Corry."

Lady Agnes leaned over to pat his hand. "As if we'd do anything less than our best for her, Reynold. Rest easy now, for she's in good hands and we're delighted to have her."

He raised her hand to his lips and kissed it fondly. "Bless you, Agnes. I bid you all a good night, then."

Her father's landau had long since gone when Corralie awoke. The nearly full moon shone brightly into the strange room and for a moment she could not think where she was. She felt inordinately drowsy, and beyond that drowsiness her head still ached and her body felt uncomfortably stiff. She lay there, waiting for the heavy, drugged sleep to drift back over her. The light footsteps were what had aroused her. Dainty steps, as if someone was dancing in the room above—— Tap. Tap-tap. Tap-tap. Corralie couldn't keep her eyes open any more.

4

Lady Agnes set the tray down beside the bed and smiled at Corralie. "Did you sleep well, my dear?"

"Yes, thank you."

"How do you feel now?"

"As if I'd just journeyed nonstop from Scotland in a stagecoach."

"Oh, I can just imagine what you mean. Now then, sit up and I'll put some extra pillows behind you. There now. My, that nightdress of Catti's suits you well."

"It's very kind of her."

"You can tell her that yourself in a little while, for she's coming to sit with you. She—er, she's been a little unwell recently."

"I'm sorry to hear that."

"Don't be—she's delighted at the cause of her illness."

"She's with child?"

"So it would appear from all the signs. She's very pleased, except that her husband isn't here with her."

"Where is he?"

"I'm not sure. Abroad somewhere, I believe."

Lady Agnes looked out the window. "It's another beautiful day. You must have brought the sunshine from London with you, Corralie. Good heavens, the *Fair Maid* is close to the end of Selney Bill. I always thought—— Well, I must have been wrong."

"What?"

"Well, it's low water and that cutter is right in the channel between Selney rocks and the end of the bill itself. I was always under the impression that the channel there was unnavigable at low tide."

"It is." Corralie set the tray aside and slipped from the bed, wincing as every joint in her body complained. With one hand against the bruise on her forehead, she stood next to Agnes to look across at the distant headland. Sure enough, the unmistakable lines of Lawrence's racing cutter were easy to make out. To the left of her was the headland itself, and to the right the jagged rocks.

"She's aground, Lady Agnes."

"Now don't get yourself into a tizzy. She hasn't broken up or anything, Corralie, even *I* can see that. Now listen, Madoc went into Chacehampton early this morning, and when he comes back he will no doubt know what has happened. Get back into that bed this instant." Lady Agnes shooed the reluctant Corralie back to the bed.

The door opened and Catti stood there, her face very pale and her eyes ringed with shadow. Her high-bosomed gown of soft gray silk did little to enhance her fragile looks.

"Ah, Catti, my dear, are you feeling a little better now?"

"Yes, thank you, Aunt Agnes. I'm so sorry to be such a nuisance."

"Nonsense, sweeting, morning sickness cannot be helped. Now then, you haven't met Corralie before, have you? Corralie, this is my niece Lady Catherine Vaughan—you've heard me mention her time and time again in the past."

"Yes, of course. How do you do, Lady Catherine."

"Catti. Please. And it's Lady Catherine Beauchamp, Aunt Agnes." The girl held her aunt's eyes for a moment. "Not Lady Catherine Vaughan. Not any more."

Lady Agnes raised her eyebrows and said nothing. Catti sat down on the edge of Corralie's bed.

Corralie looked at her. "You're not a bit like your brother, are you?"

Catti smiled. "Oh, Madoc's most definitely the black sheep and I'm the fleecy lamb, as they say. What were you looking at from the window just now?"

Lady Agnes looked out again. "Young Lord Kendal's cutter seems to be aground off the bill."

"Aground, you say? Will that not keep him from sailing for a while?" Catti twisted her handkerchief nervously in her lap.

"I just hope he's all right." Corralie stared at her toast without appetite.

"Oh, there wasn't anyone on board," said Catti.

"How do you know that?"

"I—I was walking last night and saw her at her moorings close to the navy sloop. I saw the rowing boat coming into Chacehampton harbor and I'm sure Lord Kendal was in the boat." Catti avoided Corralie's eyes.

Lady Agnes straightened her mobcap in the looking glass and when satisfied smiled at the two younger women. "I must attend to my duties. Shall I tell the cook to prepare a fine duck *à l'orange* for this evening? I know that you like it, Corralie, but do you, Catti?"

"Yes, Aunt Agnes."

"I'll leave you to your talking then, ladies." Her heavy skirts rustled across the polished wooden floor and the door closed behind her.

Catti smiled. "Eat up your toast, Corralie, or it will be cold and the butter will be dreadful."

"I'm not really hungry."

"You are worried about Lord Kendal? Please don't be, for I am sure he's safe on shore."

"I pray you are right."

"You—er, you were very friendly with him, weren't you? I mean, as children?"

"Yes. We shared the same tutor until Lawrence left for Eton, and then we only saw each other during the holidays."

"He is to marry Averil Tindling, I believe."

"Yes. On the first of August. My birthday."

"She made a fine catch, didn't she?"

"The finest in England," whispered Corralie before she could halt herself. She smiled quickly at Catti. "Forget that I said that."

"Was it Miss Tindling's notion to set the date on your birthday?" asked Catti gently.

"Yes."

"That was unkind of her."

"It was meant to be, I do assure you. There is little love lost between Averil and myself. But the victory is hers, fair and square."

"I have met Lord Kendal only once. He is very charming and good-looking. But tell me, how was he wounded? I noticed that he walked with a cane."

"He was wounded at the Pass of Maya in Spain last summer."

"Ah—a dashing cavalry officer!"

"No, actually. He was in the Thirty-ninth Regiment—it's been a Dorset regiment since oh-seven now, and besides, he has always worshiped Colonel O'Callaghan and wanted to serve with him."

"But now he is invalided out?"

"They lost ten officers and one hundred and seventy-five men at Maya. I thank God that Lawrence was only wounded."

"The French lost two thousand," said Catti. Then she smiled. "You love him very much, don't you?"

Corralie flushed. "I have no right to love him anymore, and so must learn to live with it. But it's very hard. Where is your husband, Catti? Why isn't he here with you?"

"Charles is—with the army. Abroad. But I think—I hope—I shall see him again very soon now."

"What is he like? To look at I mean?"

"He is a little older than me, younger than Madoc, not very tall, with very bright blue eyes and dark brown hair. And he is thin—his fellow officers call him Skinny. Skinny Beauchamp." She smiled. "He doesn't know yet that he is to be a father."

"I'm happy for you, Catti."

"Would that I felt a little better than I do, but I am sick so often. I know that everyone is sick for the first three or four months, but still, I'm so very, very sick. Do you think everything is all right with me, Corralie?"

Corralie smiled and put her hand over the girl's fingers. "Of course, it is most likely because you are missing your Charles so much. You need him with you now, and then everything will be all right. And anyway, when the four months are past you will begin to positively blossom."

"My mother died giving birth to me——which does not help my miseries now." Catti smiled then. "You are good for me, Corralie. Listen, that's Madoc coming. I recognize his step. Madoc, we're in here."

He came in, his riding crop swinging against his polished hessians. "Good morning, Miss Somerford. I trust this new day finds you feeling better."

"Yes, thank you." She looked at him with something of surprise, for he was so much more good-looking than she remembered from the evening before. And every inch straight from Brooks' or White's. She had seen no man more handsome during her stay in London. Whatever was a Corinthian like Sir Madoc Vaughan doing here at Webley Castle? But then she thought of Lawrence again. "Sir Madoc, you have been into Chacehampton this morning?"

"Yes."

"The *Fair Maid* is aground."

"Kendal's little tub? Yes. Her line broke, I believe."

"And Lawrence?"

"His Lordship was safely ashore at the time, wining and dining at Harry Tindling's house. With his ladylove." He smiled blandly. "Tindling is having the cutter brought into the harbor at high tide, and she is to be—er, hauled out and slipped, I believe the phrase runs."

"Harry is the finest boat builder in Dorset," said Corralie.

"And the biggest rogue, from all accounts."

"I hope you are not a secret Revenue man, Sir Madoc."

"Hardly. Do I look it?"

"Hardly." She smiled at him.

"I'm relieved to hear it. Oh, by the way, did you know that your father's old friend Captain Chadwick is in Chacehampton?"

"I haven't seen him since I was a child."

Catti looked at Madoc. "It is the *Janus*, then?"

"Yes."

Corralie glanced at Catti, for the girl had commenced twisting her handkerchief again. She seemed so on edge and tense. So frightened, almost. "What's wrong, Catti? Do you feel unwell?"

"No. No, I'm quite well, thank you. If you will excuse me, I'll go to my room for a while."

Madoc opened the door and then looked back at Corralie. "Your father charged me to tell you that your horse is safe and well—it did, as you said it would, return to its stable."

"What is my father going to do with Bracken? Did he say?" Her eyes were large and anxious.

He crossed the room and took her hand, raising it to his lips gently. "Your mount is safe from misfortune, Miss Somerford. That I promise you." He smiled. "And now I suggest you lie back for a while, for if you are too active my aunt will be up here with a selection of foul herbs with which to dose you. No doubt there are enough planets in fortunate aspect to enable her to change the botanical brew every hour or so."

The moment was broken by sounds from the floor above. Footsteps crossed the room, pacing back and forward.

"Who is that up there, Sir Madoc?"

"Oh—one of the maids I expect. The rooms on the floor above are quite empty."

When he had gone, Corralie lay back on the lacy pillows, staring up at the ceiling where the footsteps continued their restless pacing. One of the maids? A maid who just walked up and down, from one end of a room to the other?

5

The castle was quiet in the drowsy afternoon sunshine. Corralie sat miserably by the window looking out across the calm sea. Lawrence had not come to see her. Surely he knew by now that she was unwell? Averil wouldn't want him to come, but would he allow Averil's wishes to influence him that much? Would he? Corralie took a long, shaking breath. She must put Lawrence Kendal from her mind. He had chosen Averil and that must be the end of it. Except—— She lowered her eyes to the gardens beneath the window. *Except that I still love him——*

The beautiful grounds sloped away to the low rocky cliff above Webley Bay. The lawns were freshly rolled and Lady Agnes's gardeners were busy with the rose beds lining the western path. Close to the wall of the castle stood the line of beehives, and in front of them walked Lady Agnes and Catti. Lady Agnes carried a basket and she paused by the formal herb beds, which were her pride and joy. Her mobcap, as always, was lopsided, and she absent-mindedly pulled it straight while still thoughtfully surveying the herbs. Catti stifled a yawn, and Corralie was forced to smile.

The old lady took out her handkerchief and held it high in the breeze, after which she turned her back firmly to the direction of the wind and crouched to gather the herbs. With her left hand she plucked the fennel and rosemary, a feat which took her a little time as she was right-handed. Corralie watched fondly, for she had witnessed this ceremony before. But Catti seemed absolutely amazed. One of the gardeners called to the old lady fiercely.

"Not *now!* Can't you see I'm busy? Catti, go and see what he wants. I must not be distracted or the herbs will lose their potency. Go on now, girl. *Diawch!* I'm surrounded by fools and flibbertigibbets!"

Across the open sea air drifted the sound of St. James's church bells. Corralie closed the window to shut out the sound. In nine weeks' time, Lawrence would marry Averil at St. James's.

Somewhere on the floor above a window banged in the breeze. One of the maids must have left it open.

She pulled Catti's dainty lace wrap around her shoulders and opened the door of her room. The passageway was deserted. Again the window clattered on the floor above, and she slipped along toward the door leading to the stairs. It squeaked a little as she opened it, and the cool air from the enclosed stairwell swept out over her like a cold breath. She stood there for a moment in surprise, for the maids did little if any work beyond this door. There were heavy cobwebs gracing the ancient, uneven stone walls and steps, and high above she could see the smoke-stained timbers of the roof itself, blackened by the fires of centuries. A draught crept over her, making her shiver, and again she heard the banging of the window. It was louder now, echoing on the lonely stone where there was not a single carpet or tapestry.

Soon she had reached the passage that ran parallel with that on the floor below. The doors were closed, their ironwork rusty and unused. Except for the one directly over her own room. It stood open, and on the floor beyond she could see a shadow billowing on the floorboards. The window swung again and the billowing sank away as the curtains fell back into place.

Corralie felt unaccountably nervous as she approached the door, but there could be no one there, for who would allow such an irritating banging to continue without closing the window?

Sunlight drenched the room, and as Corralie stepped inside, a seagull glided past the open window, screeching so loudly that she thought for a moment that her heart would stop. She closed the window and then looked around the empty room. A carved sandalwood chest stood against one wall, and the only other thing in the room apart from that was a huge portrait of a young man in hussar uniform, riding a white horse.

She went closer, staring up at him. It was Charles Beauchamp, Catti's husband, for his name was written at the base of the golden frame. His uniform was navy blue, crusted with golden braid, and its facings and cuffs were dark red. There was a white plume in his busby and a blue and gold sash around his waist. A blue pelisse trimmed with black fur was worn casually around his narrow shoulders, and his sabretache and sword were finely decorated. The horse's shabrack was of leopardskin lined with red velvet and there was an air of movement and vigor about the whole portrait, from Charles's thin, animated face to the capering hooves of the horse. She surveyed the portrait. Why was it hidden away up here? And that uniform—— It was like the one worn by the officers at Lady Astrid's ball in London, and yet at the same time there was something different about it.

She whirled around in alarm as slow footsteps began to ascend the stairs from the floor below, and the sun chose that moment to pass behind a small cloud. The room went dark. Her heart thundered as the footsteps came along the passage to the very room where she stood, and then an even darker shadow filled the doorway. She almost squeaked with alarm.

Madoc looked at her in surprise. "Miss Somerford? Did you think I was Old Nick himself?"

She felt foolish. "The sun went behind a cloud and I heard footsteps; and this place is so very *eerie.*"

"That I grant you," he said. "But what on earth enticed you up here?"

"The window was banging."

"Two souls with but one thought. Did you see Charles's portrait?"

"Yes. But why is it kept up here?"

"My aunt does not particularly approve of Charles. For one reason or another."

Corralie would have liked to probe further, but manners precluded such nosiness. "He is very dashing."

"Is not every cavalry officer?"

"Which regiment is he in?"

"Do not ask such questions of the uninitiated, Miss Somerford, for I have little idea. One hussar looks very much like another, don't you think?" He smiled quickly.

"I suppose you're right," she replied, but she could not help thinking it odd that he did not know which regiment his brother-in-law served in.

"Come—I have a decided dislike for spiders and

there are by far too many of them abounding here." He gave her his arm.

On the carpeted, polished floor below, he closed the rusty door and shut out the cobwebs and desolation.

She stood by a narrow window that looked over the land behind the castle, and she could see the Five Warriors high on Bascombe Heath. A movement caught her eye and she looked down at the rough meadow at the foot of the castle mound. Some horses cantered playfully through the long grass, prancing and plunging as if just released from confinement in some stable. Her eyes were drawn to the dun mare leading them. Madoc came to stand beside her.

"Sir Madoc, whose horses are those?"

"They are mine."

"And the dun mare?"

"Yes. Her name is Pippit and she is the sole offspring of the brute that threw my father to his death ten years ago, thus leaving my good self to carry on the family name."

"You wouldn't consider selling her, would you?" She did not take her eyes from the thoroughbred as it broke into a stretched gallop along the smooth meadow.

"I might be persuaded."

"Could I persuade you?" She turned at last.

"Oh, Miss Somerford, I am absolutely sure that you could." He smiled at her.

She flushed. "You tease——"

"No, I am not teasing you. Oh, by the way, I have some news for you. A message was delivered a short while ago to the effect that Lord Kendal intends visiting you this evening."

She forgot Pippit. "This evening?"

"I believe each day only has one evening."

"Will that be all right? I mean, I am only a guest here——"

"*Only* a guest? Miss Somerford, my good aunt thinks that you can do no wrong—unlike my black-hearted self. Think no more of it. Lord Kendal will be made more than welcome, I am sure." He bowed slightly and left her standing by the window.

Alone in the corridor, she twirled around, hugging herself, her eyes shining. Lawrence was coming. After all these months, she would at last be seeing him again.

6

For the hundredth time she examined the folds of the clotidienne gown. The ribbon-striped satin shone turquoise and white in the evening sunlight pouring through the window of Catti's room.

Catti smiled. "It hangs as well now as ever it will, Corralie, please believe me."

"You don't think the cherryderry?"

"No, I don't. Red is not your color—well, not that bright red, anyway. Here, put on these velvet slippers. They go well with that gown, I think."

"It's not too short?"

"Is it not the fashion this year to show one's ankles? Stop fussing and do as you are told, Miss Somerford," said Catti with mock sternness.

She seemed gay and happy this evening, thought Corralie as she put on the dainty velvet slippers, full of an excitement that quivered just below the surface, lending her pale face a vivacity that the early months of pregnancy could not overcome.

"Now then," said Catti as the slippers were fastened, "a little touch of rouge, don't you think?"

"I use Portuguese rouge," said Corralie doubtfully, for she liked only that one pale pink color.

"So do I. Here." Catti pushed the rough little dish across the dressing table. "Did not Bella dress your hair prettily? I confess to thinking she is a miracle worker with my hair."

"But you have such lovely hair."

"It's willful—to curl is against its religion, I fancy."

Corralie laughed and looked at her reflection in the looking glass. Her hair was piled on top of her head in a mass of small curls, falling in long ringlets down the back.

Catti smiled. "*Very* French, *oui?* All the rage."

"*À la mode* with a vengeance. Perhaps I *am* too English in my toilet."

"No, you aren't, of course you aren't! It's just that Bella is French and believes firmly that every other nation of this earth is clueless on dress and toilet. She is such an excellent maid that I do not dare to argue for fear of losing her."

"How did you come by her?"

"Oh—luck." Catti picked up her tortoiseshell comb and ran her fingers along the teeth.

"There, I am complete. Does it look well?"

"It does. Listen, is that not someone driving over the drawbridge now?"

They heard the distinctive clattering of a single horse drawing a light carriage.

"Yes, it's Lawrence's cabriolet." Corralie took a final glance at her reflection.

"Madoc will take him to the gardens——shall we join them there?"

The gardens smelled of roses and herbs, and as the two women stepped beneath the low gateway in the stone wall they saw the seagulls winging low over the cliffs, and beyond them the crimson of the evening sea. The sun was blood-red, touching the rambling white roses and turning them to pink.

The bees droned in the hives as Corralie and Catti passed them and crossed the daisied lawn to where the two men stood by the cliff path.

Lawrence leaned on his cane, his fair head bowed thoughtfully as he listened to Madoc. He looked almost frail in a biscuit-colored coat and dark blue breeches.

He turned suddenly as if he sensed her presence, and across the sweep of the lawn he smiled at her. "Corry?"

"Lawrence."

He caught her hand and pulled her close, kissing her cheek. "Sweet Lord, Corry, what have you been up to, to frighten us all like this? But you are all right now?" He touched the bruise on her forehead gently.

"Well on the road to recovery." She knew that she was shaking and she hid her hands in the folds of clotidienne.

"London suited you?"

"I prefer it back here."

His arm tightened around her and the jeweled pin in his cravat was hard against her cheek. "And Chacehampton isn't the same without you. I curse the day I ever gave you that horse, though. I shall find you another if I have to turn England inside out."

"There's no need to do any such thing."

"But I insist that I find you something more suitable."

"A chair, perhaps?" she said with a laugh, "Even I cannot fall from a chair!"

Madoc grinned. "A rocking chair perhaps, to give the impression of movement?"

Catti smiled. "Yes, with a sealskin cushion!"

They all laughed, and then Corralie touched Lawrence's arm. "How is the *Fair Maid?* Is there much damage?"

"Not too much, but Harry has yet to go over her properly."

"The moorings frayed?"

"With a little help from someone's knife."

She stared. "Someone deliberately cut her loose? Surely not——"

"The cut is plain enough to see, Corry. I am lucky she did not founder completely on those rocks."

"But who would do such a thing?"

"Ah, that is the thousand-pound question, is it not? I have undertaken to race an American out of Boston, that's why I'm practicing at all hours of the night and day. There's a tidy fortune resting on the outcome of the race."

"And you think he may have sabotaged her?"

"I can hardly believe it, but I can think of no other explanation."

Madoc smiled. "A doubtful crowd, these ex-Colonials, eh, Kendal?"

"Maybe—but even so, I find it hard to believe of Mathingham."

Lawrence shifted his weight awkwardly, grimacing as his leg hurt. Madoc pointed to a wooden seat beside a rambling laurel bush. "Let's sit down in comfort, Kendal. How does the wound go?"

"Too damn slowly. Your pardon, ma'am." He inclined his head to Catti.

"Please feel free to say what you wish, my lord, for I am no shrinking flower to faint away at a strong word. Besides, I think I will go inside and leave you. My apologies to you all."

"Catti, you are all right?" Madoc reached out and took his sister's hand.

"I need just to lie down a little. Forgive me, Corralie, Lord Kendal."

Lawrence bowed and Madoc kissed her hand swiftly. "Rest well, *cariad*."

Madoc waited until his sister had gone and then sat on the grass by the seat, leaning back against the pedestal of a sundial, his hands behind his head. Lawrence sat on the seat thankfully, his leg stiffly straight.

"Yattere says it will take time, but even so, I cannot reconcile to not even being able to ride a horse."

"How did it happen? The Peninsula?"

"Maya."

"You encountered Boney's General D'Erlon, then?"

"Yes. A fine general, for a *parlez-vous.*"

Madoc's eyes swung to his face. "Fine indeed. But he serves the Bourbons now, as they *all* do."

"You say that as if you suspect their motives."

"I do. No one in their right minds can surely believe Bonaparte will remain on Elba——the mighty Emperor of half Europe with one small islet to rule over? One might as well believe in flying elephants."

Lawrence smiled. "Even if he did march again, there will be few to support him."

"You don't seriously believe that?"

"Yes, I do."

"Then it's as well for the army that you are invalided out."

It was very insulting, and Corralie stared at him. "Sir Madoc!" she said, horrified.

He smiled charmingly at her. "Just Madoc will do very well, you know."

Lawrence was not smiling. "You are of course entitled to your own opinion, Vaughan."

"But not to express that opinion so forcibly as to be rude. I apologize, Kendal—the remark was uncalled for."

Corralie cleared her throat, wishing to pass over the awkwardness. "How is Averil, Lawrence?"

"In the pink——more beautiful each time I see her. Don't you think so, Vaughan?"

"Miss Tindling is very charming."

"The most beautiful creature in creation, and the sweetest angel I ever knew."

Madoc picked a long-stemmed daisy and presented it to Corralie. "That is impossible, for the lady with the best claim to those titles sits here with us now."

She flushed. "You *are* given to teasing."

"I am also given to speaking the truth on occasion."

Lawrence looked thoughtfully at Madoc, and then at Corralie. "Corry, Averil charged me to invite you to dine with us at Henarth when you are better."

With just the two of you? Never! She smiled and looked at Madoc. "Then I must have an escort, must I not, to keep an even balance at the table?"

"Yes, yes, of course——how remiss of me," said Lawrence after a moment. "You will join us, Vaughan?"

Madoc inclined his head. "I accept with alacrity—what man would turn from the prospect of escorting Miss Somerford? And now, if you will excuse me, I have work to do." He stood and bowed to them both and then strolled back up the long garden.

Lawrence watched him. "The fellow's got a notion for you, Corry."

"He was just being polite. Drawing-room manners."

"Rubbish—he was pleased as punch to accept, and you know it."

"Don't be silly," she said, flushing.

"I don't know that I like it. He's a notorious *bon vivant*, you know. Kept three mistresses at the same time, so I'm told—and got away with it for a while before they all found him out."

"You're only jealous."

He put his hand over hers. "I just don't like the fellow making up to you, that's all."

"He doesn't!"

"He would, given half the chance."

"And I might just enjoy it, given half the chance. And anyway, if you disapprove so much, why did you take me up on what I said and ask him to the dinner party?"

"You didn't leave me much choice. Besides, I can keep my eye on him at Henarth."

"And on me?"

"Yes," he said with a laugh, "if you are likely to enjoy his flattery!"

"You have a nerve, Lawrence Kendal, I'll grant you that."

"I am being the elder brother you never had."

She looked away quickly. "I have never thought of you in that light," she said softly. She could not help herself, for there was still time, he was not completely Averil's yet.

He raised her hand to his lips. "I know, Corry, but I'm sorry——" He did not finish.

His eyes were so very blue as he looked at her, and the sea breeze moved his fair hair. The painful truth was there in those blue eyes, and she could not mistake it. She lowered her eyes to hide the tears.

"No, look at me, Corry. Please. Forgive me for hurting you."

"There is nothing to forgive."

"There is—I've been guilty of wanting you both and of letting you believe I would change my mind. That was unforgivable."

"But you chose Averil, and there is the end of it."

He leaned forward and very gently kissed her on the lips. "My sweet Corry, you have not deserved me to blight your life."

The sunset was blazing in the west now. The shades of scarlet and vermilion were fading, leaving fingers of pale, clear yellow which were spreading to become a soft primrose.

"There will be rain tomorrow," she said incongruously, swallowing back the tears.

Later, when he had gone, she remained by the laurel bush, staring at the guillemots by the rocks of the bay. She heard the cabriolet drive out over the drawbridge and the tears fell down her cheeks. "Oh, Lawrence," she whispered, "why could it not have been me?"

7

Madoc slowly closed Corralie's door and turned to his sister. "She's asleep. Now you go to your room and stay there."

"But Madoc——"

"No buts. I will go down alone."

"Why can't I come? You are sure the sloop will not come? You have not lied to me?" She gripped his arm.

"Quiet," he hissed, glancing back at Corralie's door. "Aunt Agnes may sleep like the proverbial log, but I can't say how well our guest slumbers. And don't worry about the *Janus*—at ten o'clock her crew were still carousing ashore. The bos'n said they would not be going aboard before dawn if they could help it."

"But the men up on Selney Bill!"

"Have been sent an anonymous keg of something good and strong to keep them tipsy." He smiled. "But I'd still like to know why Chadwick's posted a permanent watch up there."

"You don't think——"

"Us? Well, it could be, somehow a whisper could have got out. It's more likely to be Harry

Tindling's activities. But I cannot be sure. Anyway, after tonight it won't matter anymore. Now go on, back to your room."

She hesitated and then turned, walking slowly along the passageway. At the door to the floor above she paused, smiling back at him. He said nothing as she opened it and went up the stairs to the deserted rooms above.

The night seemed heavy and close, although a breeze blew in through the open window, and Corralie could hear the steady fresh rhythm of the waves upon the pebbles of the shore. She lay there, her heart still pounding from the nightmare that had waked her. The wild, frightened galloping of her accident had reached through the night, spinning a blur of branches and leaves, and a haze of cream-colored flowers—meadowsweet. She stared at the carved ceiler of the bed, so clear in the moonlight that lay slanting across the room. Meadowsweet. And two, pale, shadowy faces.

A soft sound spread through the room. Tap. Tap-tap. Tap-tap. The dainty, dancing footsteps were coming from the room above again. The threads of the nightmare vanished into the night as Corralie slipped from the bed and picked up the lace wrap. Her velvet slippers made no sound as she left her room and went toward the stair door.

The enclosed air of the upper story smelled stale and musty as she went up. The light of a candle flickered in the room where Charles Beauchamp's portrait hung, and the little tapping steps were clearer now.

The door stood open and Corralie stared from the shadows as Catti's dancing figure set the candle jumping and shivering. Shadows reached wildly over the room, trembling across the thin, painted face of the portrait and making it seem almost alive. Catti held the man's coat against her. It was an exquisitely fashioned corbeau-colored evening coat, cut so fashionably that it would have graced the Court itself. Her cheek rested against the soft velvet color and she hummed as she danced, for all the world as if she held not just the coat but the man himself.

Corralie watched and then felt guilty at seeing something so private. Catti's great love was written on her face as she twirled. Corralie melted back along the passageway and down the stairs. On the floor below she stood for a moment by the window that looked over the meadow where the horses had been. It was then that she saw the signaling light reflected from sea in the window of the room of the wing opposite.

She hurried into her own room and there, sure enough, from her own window she saw the light out at sea. Three long flashes and then one shorter one. By the light of the full moon she saw the silhouette of the ship, still a little way off shore.

Below her, Madoc stood by the garden seat, one foot resting on its arm, the storm lantern held high as he swung it to and fro. The lights on the ship ended immediately and he put the lantern down. He put a small telescope to his eye and turned toward Selney Bill and for a long while he studied something there, and then he left the lantern and the telescope by the seat and vanished down the cliff path to the beach. Out at sea, the ship was closer, nosing slowly toward Webley Bay's narrow mouth.

Corralie hardly hesitated. She hurried down the stairs to the hallway, where the suits of armor looked menacing in the darkness. The doors of the castle stood open and as she went into the courtyard she could hear the dry rustling of the ivy leaves clinging to the walls of the ancient building.

The perfume of rosemary, mint, and sage filled the air as she passed the herb gardens, and the roses swayed seductively, the blooms heavy and sweet.

Down in the bay the ship was clear now, a three-masted lugger with white sails, all but one of which was red. She heard the rattling of the anchor chain and watched as a small boat was lowered. Down at the water's edge Madoc stood waiting.

She slipped silently down the narrow path, hidden from view by a small ravine, but at the foot of the path she halted, for the rowing boat was coming ashore very close to where she stood and Madoc was walking to meet it.

"Darnier?"

"*Oui, monsieur.*" The boat grated as it reached the shore.

"Where is he?"

"He was not there, *monsieur*. We waited, but he did not come."

Madoc was angry. "You waited! But for how long?"

"Three days, *monsieur*. Three long days and nights. Then the British Commissioner's corvette began to show an interest. We dared not wait longer. There was a frigate in Leghorn—the telegraph from Portoferraio could have trapped us. I shall not go back there, *monsieur*, it is too dangerous."

"Then you get no payment, Darnier, not one single coin!"

The other kicked angrily at the pebbles. "Would you have me endanger my ship and crew for one man?"

"You are being paid to do something you do anyway—*contrabandier!* And the sum involved more than covers three or four normal runs! You know the arrangements—you are to wait there two weeks before full moon."

Darnier looked out at the lugger and then

nodded. "Very well, once more we try. But only once. If he is not there next time, then we go and we do not come back at all. There is too much danger around that island. You attended to the *milord?*"

"Yes, he'll not be sailing for a while with a damaged hull."

"We sighted the other ship, the one by the headland over there. A sloop. We could not make out her colors. Who is she?"

"A Swedish tub," said Madoc smoothly.

Corralie's lips parted. He knew that the *Janus* was a naval vessel——

"And my friend Tindling? I do not wish to encounter him at all."

"The *Laura* is still being refitted somewhere."

"He would not take kindly to my coming to his domain."

"He will not know, will he?"

"I will go back then, *monsieur*. If he is not there, you will not see me again—there are, as you say, other fish in the sea." The Frenchman gazed around the quiet beach. "You chose well here, did you not?"

"Of necessity."

The Frenchman nodded. "Indeed—when one changes colors, one has to be circumspect. Is that not the word?"

"Yes."

Darnier climbed into the rowing boat and Madoc pushed it off on the next wave. Corralie turned and fled up the path as Madoc began to walk back toward the cliff.

In her own room again, she stood by the window and watched the lugger. Her white sails flapped gently as they were hoisted and the anchor weighed, and she moved seaward on the ebbing tide, her single red sail quite clear in the moonlight.

Corralie watched Madoc. He stood in the gardens, his head bowed and his shoulders slumped dejectedly. Then he passed from her sight into the castle.

She slipped into her bed and lay there, awake. She hardly heard the door open, but she knew that he came to stand by the bed, for she could smell the costmary on his clothes. The door closed quietly and he was gone. She opened her eyes, listening, and later she heard Catti's sad weeping.

8

Corralie sat silently the next morning as Bella dressed her hair. Hardly a sound punctuated the silence; only an occasional sniff and swallow as the French maid worked to hide the fact that she, too, had been weeping. Corralie took the freshly laundered cambric mobcap and tied its crisp ribbons beneath her chin.

"*C'est bien, Bella,*" she said, smiling. "*Merci.*"

The maid curtsied and left the room, sniffing once more as she closed the door.

Corralie stood, plucking at the gathers of the yellow seersucker gown where the strings were pulled so tightly beneath her breasts. There was an atmosphere in the castle this morning, and she could feel it even though she hadn't set foot from her own room yet. A heaviness pervaded everything, a heaviness that the lowering skies outside did little to alleviate. She looked down at the garden seat; she had been right when she said that there would be rain after so pale yellow a sky. A little of the heaviness seemed to seep from the castle and into her heart as she remembered sitting there with Lawrence. *Was it only yesterday that he told me——*

She could hear his voice even now, see the sadness in his eyes. And feel his lips so gently over hers.

She felt the tears pricking her eyes again and angrily blinked them away. She had known for months now that he had chosen Averil, why be so heartbroken over what he had said? Why? Because it had seemed so very final somehow—— With a final flick of her skirts, she left the room.

At Catti's door she halted, for it was open a little and she could see the girl's reflection in the tall gilt looking glass. Catti sat on her bed, her hands folded in her lap and her head bent. There was something so infinitely sad about the slender little figure in cream muslin that Corralie could not pass the room without going to her.

"Catti?"

The large brown eyes were red-rimmed and the thin face even more drawn than usual, and the change in her after the sparkle of the day before was so dramatic that Corralie could scarce hide her alarm. "What is wrong?" She sat beside the girl and took her cold, shaking hand. "Catti?"

"Please don't worry, Corralie, I am all right."

"No, you aren't—don't try to push me away with words like that. I can see that you are upset." And it had something to do with that French lugger in the bay last night, Corralie would have laid odds on it. Who had Madoc expected? The answer followed the question—Catti's husband, Charles Beauchamp. But if Catti would not say, then Corralie could offer little comfort, for to say anything to the girl would be to admit that she had been prying on the beach the night before.

"I—I was expecting my husband, but now I must wait at least another month to see him. I need him so much now, do you see, Corralie?"

Corralie slipped her arms around the girl's shivering shoulders. "But he will come in a month's time and then you will feel much happier, Catti."

"I pray so."

"Where is he, then?"

"Oh, somewhere in the Mediterranean, I believe." Catti looked away.

"Come down and have some breakfast—something to eat and something to drink—and it won't seem so bad."

"No, Corralie, I could not eat. I would be sick, and the thought of sitting in a room filled with the smell of food turns my stomach over. I will wait a while and then take some toast and milk a little later."

The morning gong echoed through the castle and Corralie stood. "I don't like to leave you——"

"Bella is coming to stay with me in a moment." Catti smiled. "You are very kind, Corralie. I wish——"

"Yes?"

"I wish you could be here always."

That wasn't what you were going to say—— At that moment, Bella came in and Corralie left the two together.

As she descended the stairs where the suits of polished armor stood on each landing, she wondered about what she had discovered. Charles Beauchamp had been expected last night, making an unconventional and secret landing down in the bay. From a *French* lugger, captained by a man obviously of Harry Tindling's ilk. But try as she would, she could not remember the names of the ports the Frenchman had mentioned.

She crossed the hallway with its white-washed walls and hanging crossed swords. What was going on? Why would Catti's husband travel on a French ship which would obviously have much to fear from the British navy? Her hand was on the door of the dining room when another thought suddenly struck her, so forcibly that she halted, her lips parted. What had the Frenchman asked? *"You attended to the milord?"* And Madoc had replied that he had, that the *milord* would not sail in a ship with a damaged hull. Lawrence. It had been Madoc who had cut the *Fair Maid's* moorings!

He was sitting at the table with his aunt, and he folded his napkin and stood, smiling, as Corralie went in. "Good morning, Miss Somerford. I trust you slept well."

"Very well, thank you, Sir Madoc. Good morning, Lady Agnes."

"Ah, Corralie, my dear, you are looking well this morning. Fully recovered, I fancy."

"I was thinking that I have imposed for long enough——"

"Nonsense," said the old lady, beaming. "And Doctor Yattere said that you were not to leave until *he* had given his permission."

"I do not wish to seem rude, but I am embarrassed at remaining here when as you say I am obviously well. Could we perhaps send for the doctor and let him examine me again?"

"If that is what you want, then of course, my dear. Is Drew going in to Chacehampton today, Madoc?"

"To bring the farrier, yes. He is leaving after luncheon."

"Then he shall take a message to the doctor." Lady Vaughan glanced at the footman standing so motionless by the sideboard. "This coffeepot," she said tartly, "has been standing empty for the past five minutes."

The man jumped, hurrying to the table and spiriting the silver pot from the room. The door clattered noisily behind him and Lady Vaughan took a long, quivering breath. "That man is neither efficient nor conversant with the ways of a large house."

"There are more lucrative livings to be had around here by sailing with Harry Tindling, *ma tante*," said Madoc, smiling at her.

"One would imagine an oaf like Simmonds would forget he was aboard the *Laura* and step clean off the side and into the sea! To think that I must descend to employing such a—a person!"

Corralie buttered herself some toast and spread it with lemon marmalade, watching Madoc from beneath lowered lashes. He was looking from the dining hall window which afforded a direct view down the gardens toward the bay. What was he thinking about? The lugger? Looking at him in the sane morning light, it was hard to believe that he had been responsible for the cutting loose of the *Fair Maid*. And yet—*was* it so hard? He gave the impression of being lazy, given more to the pleasures of London and soft living than to anything else; but for all that, there was something about him. Something sinister, perhaps? Was that the word——?

He felt her gaze and looked suddenly at her. "If you are determined to leave us, you will have to ride Pippit this morning or not at all, won't you?"

"Could I?" Suddenly the thought of a ride, of the wind on her face and the freedom of Bascombe Heath, seemed the prospect of paradise itself.

He nodded. "Why not? I at least feel the need to shake myself free of the cobwebs this morning. I will have Drew tack up Pippit and The Beau."

"The Beau? The Duke of Wellington's nickname?"

"The horse is named for the great Duke, yes."

"Why?"

"Because it is a brilliant tactician—the creature

knows the precise second when he is most likely to be able to unseat my good self."

She laughed, forgetting the gloom for a moment. "*All* horses have that ability, Sir Madoc."

"Madoc."

She glanced at Lady Agnes and then at him again. "Very well. Madoc."

"That is infinitely more friendly, Corralie."

"It also flouts the set rules of behavior somewhat."

"To Old Nick with rules. Now, I will have our mounts got ready. Can you be in the courtyard in, say, half an hour? Or is that rushing you somewhat?"

"I will be ready in half an hour."

"Madoc," he prompted, smiling.

"Madoc."

9

The hooves drummed satisfyingly on the grassy meadow where the shadows were muted by the stormy day. The greens of Bascombe Wood were softened, the colors blending flatly as the trees swayed to the strengthening wind. Corralie's hair was pinned and restrained beneath the beaver hat, and she wished longingly that convention did not demand that a lady's head be covered at all times. Each drum of Pippit's hooves sent the "cobwebs" Madoc had referred to spinning farther and farther away, and she delighted in the perfection of the dun mare. They cantered down the narrow lane toward the ford, and she saw the honeysuckle twisting its way over the white boughs of hawthorn. The lacy cow parsley shook in the draught of the horses' passing, and a blackbird chattered with alarm, fluttering away low over the hedges to the safety of the trees.

Madoc reined in as they reached the edge of the woods, where the wheel marks of Averil's dogcart were still plain in the soft mud. He stretched in the saddle to look up at the Five Warriors, so dramatic against the lowering sky where mushrooms of yellow-gray storm clouds were burgeoning from horizon to horizon. The wind soughed through the trees as he turned to Corralie.

"Have we time to get up there, do you think?"

"We must make time." She was not going to forego a gallop across the heath.

He caught the careworn note in her voice. "I would not have thought you needed this ride in the same way as I."

"No? Then you would be mistaken." She urged Pippit across the ford and then reined in again, turning to stare at the mossy bank with its fringe of meadowsweet. The flowers' perfume filled the little clearing.

He watched her apprehensively; pray God she wasn't remembering—— "You recall something of your fall?"

"It was here? No, I don't remember anything beyond being at the Five Warriors watching Lawrence's cutter." There was no flicker on his face when she mentioned the *Fair Maid*, she noticed; no hint of anything out of the ordinary.

Disappointed not to have drawn any reaction from him, she bent to pick a spike of meadowsweet. "It was Queen Elizabeth's favorite herb, you know—she liked to have it strewn on the floors to make the rooms smell sweet."

"*Spirea ulmaria*," he said drily.

"Meadowsweet sounds so much more pleasing."

"More romantic?"

"Less stuffy."

He grinned. "'That's something I am not. Come on, we are going to get wet, but perhaps not completely drenched if we ride on now." The wind had risen, stirring his thick, black hair and snatching at his cravat. He glanced up as the first heavy drops of rain began to fall and then he pushed his top hat more firmly on his head.

The rain pattered noisily on the wide, flat leaves of the wild rhubarb at the water's edge and left dark spots on Corralie's riding habit as she urged Pippit after The Beau.

The clouds were so low now that the horses moved through mist over the heath, and the gorse and heather were damp and moisture-hung. Corralie wanted to laugh out loud as her beaver hat was at last dislodged from its pins, falling unheeded to the ground. Her hair was wet and so was her face, and Pippit's black mane clung to her sweating neck as they rode through the ghostly standing stones. On and on they rode until at last they dropped down beneath the cloud and on to the edge of the heath, and there Madoc reined in.

"No more cobwebs," he laughed. His hair was wet, tightening into curls, and his hat dripped rivulets down his back and shoulders, leaving his once magnificent cravat a sadly collapsed heap of white cloth.

"If you had earrings," she said, "you would look the perfect gypsy!"

"I doubt that the ladies of Almack's would let *you* over the threshold either!" He stood in the stirrups, staring across Chacehampton Bay toward Selney Bill where the naval sloop *Janus* lay at anchor.

Corralie saw how closely he surveyed the distant craft, and then how he gazed up at the very end of the hill, where the old seventeenth-century fortifications could be made out against the skyline.

"Would you like to ride to the end of the bill, then?" she asked, her voice almost drowned by the noise of the rain. Behind them, thunder rumbled over the mist-hidden heath.

"I will if you will," he said, grinning.

"I take the offer back."

"I thought you would."

They rode on, more slowly now for it was hardly possible to get any wetter than they already were. Steam rose from the horses' flanks and the The Beau's neck was foam-flecked.

A post chaise was rattling along the road ahead of them from the direction of Dorchester, the yellow-jacketed post boy looking wet and miserable as he urged his tired team toward Chacehampton. As Madoc and Corralie drew alongside to pass the carriage, someone looked out. It was Averil.

She tapped the grille at the front of the chaise and it swayed to a standstill. Corralie's spirits fell, for she had no desire to speak with Averil.

"Good day, Corralie. Sir Madoc." Averil's eyes betrayed nothing as she smiled at him.

"Miss Tindling." He bowed forward in the saddle, smiling in return.

Corralie was painfully aware of the dreadful sight she must make. Surely she looked more like a drowned rat than Reynold Somerford's wealthy daughter?

Averil spoke to Madoc. "Out on such a day, Sir Madoc?"

"I might say the same to you, Miss Tindling."

The girl's eyes slid to Corralie. "I have been to Dorchester, to purchase items for the wedding."

Madoc gathered The Beau's reins. "We, on the other hand, have merely been out riding for pleasure. Corralie wished to ride Pippit."

Corralie nodded stiffly. "And now perhaps we should go back or we will take some terrible fever at the very least." She urged Pippit on down the muddy lane, splashing through the puddles that had already accumulated in the ruts.

Averil looked up at Madoc. "My—my father is going out tonight." She flushed immediately, knowing that she had been extremely forward.

He smiled. "A visit to your house would be a little ill-advised, surely?"

"I would like to see you again." The flush deepened.

"Then of course I will come." He touched his top hat and then turned his mount after Corralie. As he rode along the dripping lane, he smiled; an invitation into the very nest of Harry Tindling——

It was still raining as they dismounted at Webley Castle, handing the reins of their tired mounts to the waiting grooms. They ran across the blustery courtyard to the doorway, halting beneath the old stone porch, laughing at having at last reached shelter.

He caught her hand, taking off his top hat. "Perhaps there is only one right way to end this morning." He bent his head to kiss her, and his lips tasted of the rain.

She said nothing, but as the butler opened the heavy double doors she went inside, her skirts clinging to her legs as she hurried toward the stairs.

Madoc watched her. Surely that was one step closer he had come to old Somerford's thousands? He took a coin from his waistcoat pocket and tossed it in the air, catching it. He grinned at the butler. "Heads. I win," he murmured.

10

Dr. Yattere inspected the bruise carefully. "It has healed well—very well indeed."

Lady Agnes raised her eyebrow. "Of course, hyssop is an excellent remedy."

"No doubt," grunted the doctor, unimpressed.

"Are you telling me that bruise would be so well recovered had I not used the herb?"

"One cannot say, can one? There was no control experiment to give the lie to anything you might say, madam."

She raised her chin fiercely. "That, sir, is just the sort of vapid answer I would expect from a physician!"

He snapped his bag shut angrily. "You are well, Corralie, and may return whenever you wish."

"Doctor Yattere, did you speak to my father about Bracken?"

"I did indeed."

"And?"

"And I understand that he has already disposed of the brute."

She stared, her eyes huge. "Disposed?"

He smiled. "Not at the slaughterhouse. I gather it

has gone back to Lord Kendal and that your father is in the process of purchasing some other mount for you." He put on his hat and bowed stiffly to Lady Agnes. "I bid you good day, my lady."

"Good day, sir."

Catti smiled as she and Corralie were left alone. "They bristle like cats, don't they?"

"They always do. Catti, are you a little better now?"

"Yes. It was just the first disappointment."

It's more than that. Corralie outwardly accepted the explanation, but inwardly she knew that there was far more to Catti's misery than mere disappointment. "Catti, now that I am to go back to my home, I must thank you again for your kindness to me."

"It was no more than you would do for me."

"Nonetheless——"

"I enjoyed your company more than you can know, Corralie, for it is a little lonely here with just my aunt. Oh, Madoc does his best, but it is not the same as having another woman to talk with."

"You will come to call upon me, won't you?"

"If you promise to come back here sometimes."

Corralie hugged her. "Of course I will, for I trust and hope that we are friends now."

"If I stand next in the line, will you hug me as well?" Madoc closed the door and smiled at her.

It was the first time she had seen him since the end of the ride that morning, and she flushed quickly. "That would not be proper, would it?"

"How discriminatory."

Catti prodded him. "You will embarrass her, Madoc. Stop it."

"It is one of my Libran failings, as Aunt Agnes would say."

"She would also say that Librans are supposed to have tact, charm, and diplomacy—something must have gone sadly wrong with the planets at your birth." Catti smiled fondly at him.

He put his hand to his sister's chin. "Are you scolding me?"

"With great glee."

"Tiger." He looked at her, "You are all right, now?"

"Yes."

"Good." He pretended to tweak her nose and then looked at Corralie. "I gather that you are indeed leaving us today."

"I cannot outstay my welcome."

"That you would never do."

Catti made to leave. "Oh, Madoc, while I think of it, could you take me for a drive this evening after dinner? The storm is over and I would so like a drive along the cliff road."

"Forgive me this once, Catti, but I cannot."

"Why?"

"I have—an appointment."

"Oh." Catti's eyes flew to Corralie and then she hurried from the room.

Corralie felt uncomfortable. "I do believe she imagines your appointment to be with me."

"No, she doesn't. She wrongly imagines it to be with a Chacehampton demirep." He poured two glasses of wine and pushed one into her hand. "I trust my behavior earlier today has not offended you."

"I behaved poorly."

"You? I rather thought that I was the one guilty of poor behavior."

"I should at the very least have stamped my pretty foot."

"But you did not."

"No, which fact it does not please me to remember."

"Ah, but it pleases me."

She smiled. "You are too practiced, Madoc Vaughan."

"A lifetime's study of the art must surely be rewarded by a little brilliance."

She laughed. "It is impossible to be angry with you, isn't it?"

"I hope so. Corralie, would you stamp your pretty foot now if I asked your permission to call upon you?"

She looked down at her glass. "You are Lady Agnes's nephew and therefore free to call upon me."

"I will be content with that."

They both heard the cabriolet rattling into the courtyard and through the window saw the crimson vehicle draw up and Lawrence climb down.

"Well, Kendal, I do believe," said Madoc. "Shall we see what he wants?"

Lawrence's cane tapped on the stone floor of the great hall and Lady Agnes held out her hands warmly. "Lord Kendal, what an unexpected pleasure this is."

"Lady Agnes."

"The way you dashed into Webley a moment ago must surely mean that you are a high-flying man-about-town of the first order."

"I trust so," he smiled, sitting down in the chair she indicated.

"And your poor leg, how is it coming along?"

"Slowly but surely."

"Can you ride yet?"

"No, but I should be in the saddle by the next hunting season."

"One surely hopes so. Ah, Corralie, Madoc, see? We have a visitor."

Madoc held up a hand to stop Lawrence rising. "Good afternoon, Kendal, how's your cutter?"

"She's to be hauled out and slipped tomorrow, but I don't think her hull's damaged too badly."

Corralie glanced at Madoc, but he was smiling innocuously. "Let us hope so. Have you any notion yet who did it?"

"None at all. Chadwich says that his watch saw nothing that night. The *Janus* was moored close by, but the first anyone knew was when the *Fair Maid* drifted past on the ebb tide." Lawrence looked at Corralie and smiled. "I came to take you home."

"How did you know?"

"I came upon Yattere a short while ago and asked him how you were. Have you much baggage to take back?"

"Only one rather wet and crumpled riding habit—Catti has very kindly let me wear one of her gowns and a pelisse."

"Ah, yes, I gather you were caught in the storm this morning." Lawrence looked briefly at Madoc. "I trust the ride was worth the soaking."

Madoc smiled deliberately at Corralie. "Oh, most definitely."

She felt an embarrassed color creep over her. "I—I think I will find Catti to say goodbye, then."

Madoc hurried to open the door for her.

The cabriolet spun along the lane toward the first houses on the edge of the town. "I told Vaughan we'd dine on the fifth of June. Half past nine for ten. It will be dark then for the lanterns. That suit, Corry?"

"I know of no reason why not. Why are you taking me this way? I thought you were taking me home."

"I thought you'd like to see the *Fair Maid*."

Berthed right alongside Harry Tindling's boatyard, no doubt—— She retied the ribbons of

Catti's pink straw bonnet and prayed that there would be no sign of Averil.

The wheels of the cabriolet were noisy on the cobbled quayside where the fishing boats were moored and their catch was being brought ashore in baskets. The seagulls screamed hopefully overhead, perching on masts and rigging and being driven away if they became too persistent.

Corralie gazed around her fondly. She loved this place. Her glance fell on a new name over what had once been a ships' chandler's store. "Oh, Lawrence! A dressmaker!"

"Miss Yelverton? Yes, I gather from Averil that she is very good indeed. Got a great many French patterns and a wondrous store of cloths and lace. Averil's getting her wedding gown made there, anyway, so she must think the woman's good."

The cabriolet drew up by Harry Tindling's rambling old house beside which was the boatyard. The keel of a schooner was being laid and the bell rang as they arrived for the men to take a well-earned rest. The sudden silence after all the hammering and singing was quite startling as Lawrence helped Corralie down. "Harry's yard is doing brisk business, I fancy," he said, his eyes moving over the house for a sign of Averil.

"All Harry's enterprises seem to be doing well, I gather."

He smiled. "I prefer to pretend I do not know about his other activities—for a lord to knowingly marry a smuggler's daughter would bring me a notoriety I would not care for."

"So you blink your big blue eyes and look the picture of innocence?"

"Something like that."

"Well, you've fooled half the people in Chacehampton, anyway, for they all believe you to be ignorant of the truth."

He smiled. "People often appear to believe that of me, Corry."

She looked away quickly. "Where is the *Fair Maid?*"

"In the side quay over there."

He helped her across the gangplank and onto the well-scrubbed deck of the racing cutter. "She'd run in well, too, damn it—if I could find out who'd cut her loose I'd hang him at Chacehampton crossroads, so help me I would." Lawrence bent to push a coil of rope aside.

"Do you still have the same crew?" she asked, to change the conversation.

"Yes, all thirty of them. We'll see that Boston pirate off the seven seas yet." He bent carefully down into the cabin, grimacing at the persistent stiffness of his leg.

"Could you see the *Laura* off, Lawrence?"

"Harry's got that craft so close-hauled at times with the cargo he carries that he tempts Providence, don't you know."

"He's not come unstuck yet," she said.

"Yet. Ah, now I recall stringing a good bottle of Moselle over the side last night—— Yes, here it is." Lawrence pulled on the rope that hung from the cabin down into the chilly water of the harbor, and on the end of it was tied a dripping bottle of wine. "That's as chilled as anything outside an icehouse."

"This will be my second glass of wine this afternoon—I shall be tipsy if I continue at this rate."

"Second?"

"I took a drink with Madoc."

"Madoc, is it? So friendly in so short a time?"

She looked up at the edge on his voice. "And if we are?"

"It lacks—propriety."

"And what business is it of yours?" she asked softly.

"None, I suppose. But, damn it all, Corry, he's a blasted fortune hunter."

"There are those to say that of Averil!"

He banged the bottle on the table. "Blast you for saying that, Corry."

"And blast you, too, Lawrence Kendal! You seem to think it perfectly in order to speak to me like that, but only one retort from me and you cannot take it!"

He searched for something to open the bottle with and she pushed the corkscrew across the table. He picked it up and looked at her. "If Vaughan is what I think he is, and if he gets you to the altar, Corry, he'll eventually control your fortune. He'll be your lord and master, and you should see it like that when he speaks so seductively to you—he's nothing but the damned serpent in the eternal garden!"

"That's not much of a compliment to me!" she snapped.

"I did not mean it like that. I meant that a man like Vaughan cannot possibly contemplate pursuing anyone who is not rich in her own right."

"I am not being pursued."

"Oh, come on, Corry—he's damned open enough about it."

"A point in his favor, surely! To be open! You were offering me a glass of Moselle."

"If I'm so wrong about him, why are you blushing so?"

"If you don't leave the subject alone, Lawrence, I shall go ashore and find my own way home."

"Why are you so thorny about the fellow?"

She whirled around angrily. "*Me?* Give me patience! Lawrence, it is you who are the bear in all this, not me. I accept that you neither like him nor approve of any friendship I might have of him. Let us leave it at that. All right? Just as I accept your bethrothal to Averil while neither liking her nor approving of the match."

He took a long, angry breath. "I just don't want—I don't want you to turn to someone like Vaughan because—because——"

She felt both angry and humiliated. "You think I would let myself be caught on the rebound from losing you? You flatter yourself."

The cabin was suddenly silent, and she could hear her own heart thundering and her pulses racing. He closed his eyes. "Oh, Corry——" He held out his hand and after a moment she took it, allowing him to draw her into his arms. He rested his cheek against hers. "Don't let's quarrel. I'm in the wrong and we've both said things that were better not said."

She drew away, unable to bear being in his arms like that. "The wine——" She poured two glasses of the chilled wine. "We'll both pledge to forget this quarrel."

He raised his glass and smiled at her. "Can't bear quarreling with you, Corry. You nearly always get the last word. I should damn well know that by now."

He looked beyond her suddenly, out through the harbor entrance to where they could see the *Janus.* "They're signalling again. See? Up there on Selney Bill. They flash a signal down to the sloop every so often and she acknowledges. I've been watching carefully, and it always happens the same way—after a while a ship of some sort appears on the horizon. They're watching for something."

The *Belle Marie?* The thought passed through Corralie's head so swiftly that she hardly knew it was there. Was the *Janus* there to watch for Harry Tindling's smuggling cutter? Or was she there to watch for the French lugger?

They both heard the footsteps on the gangplank at the same time.

"Lawrence?" It was Averil.

Corralie's heart sank and she drank a little more of the Moselle, smiling nervously at Lawrence.

"Down here, Averil—we're down here," he called.

"We?" Averil came daintily down into the cabin, radiant in her green-and-white checked silk dress. Her smile almost froze as she saw Corralie, but then she smiled warmly at Lawrence. "I saw the cabriolet."

He went to her, kissing her warmly on the cheek. "I hope I might see you. I thought we might dine together tonight."

Her smile faltered momentarily. "Tonight? Oh—I am expecting my cousin from Abbotsworth tonight, Lawrence. Could we not make it tomorrow? Oh, please don't look like that—so chagrined."

"It's difficult when I *am* chagrined. You know that, eh, Corry? That I can't hide me damned feelings?"

"You never could." She smiled as pleasantly as she could. "Hello again, Averil."

"Corralie. You are dried from your ride?"

"It would appear so."

"Was Sir Madoc's horse as fine as you'd thought?"

"A magnificent beast—would that she were mine."

Averil smiled stiffly. "Can you not persuade him to sell her to you?"

Corralie flushed at the unintentionally apt words. "If I were him, I would not part with her for a fortune."

Lawrence looked a little nervously from one to the other and then out of the window again as the signals passed between the sloop and the men on

the headland. "They're at it again. Damn it, I'd
love to know what it's all about."

Both Corralie and Averil were glad of the diver-
sion. Averil looked up at the flashing light. "My father says they signal whenever a ship appears
beyond the horizon."

"Yes, I've noticed that."

Averil glanced at Corralie. "I wonder what
they're looking out for?"

For the first time a vague drift of humor passed
between the two women, for both were thinking of
Harry's smuggling cutter, which Corralie knew was
tidily laid up in the tidal reaches of the river that
passed through the grounds of Reynold Somerford's house.

Lawrence smiled blandly. "You might find out,
Corry—your father's invited old Chadwick to dine
some time this week."

"Oh lord—has he?" Corralie pulled a wry face,
for as she remembered him, "good old Chadders"
was rather heavy going at a dinner party. "He
thinks women, like children, should be seen but not
heard. He practically banishes me from the dinner
table before the final course has been served!"

Lawrence grinned. "And quite right, too."

"Toad! Is he not a toad, Averil?" Corralie put
out a tentative feeler of friendship—for if she was
to retain Lawrence's goodwill, she must be at peace
with Averil.

"Very definitely," answered Averil. She would
have accepted the olive branch more sweetly had it
not been for that morning ride in the rain—— A
twist of unreasonable jealousy stirred in her, a confusing jealousy. She knew that it was madness to be
so fascinated by Madoc Vaughan, and yet she
could not help herself. And Lawrence was so terri-
bly and boringly *nice!*

He picked up his cane as the chimes of St.

James's sounded six. "Lord, Corry, I'll not get you back before Reynold has his dinner set out. Averil, are you sure you cannot turn away your damned cousin this evening?"

"She—she will be on her way by now, Lawrence. But tomorrow? I promise to keep tomorrow evening for you." She smiled nervously, and Corralie watched her curiously.

Averil remained in the cabin after the cabriolet had gone. She looked at the half-full bottle of Moselle and two empty glasses, and then at her engagement ring. She twisted the ring on her finger; the fictitious visit of her equally fictitious cousin was the first lie she had told Lawrence. The first out-and-out lie. She bit her lip and then climbed the steps out onto the cutter's decks.

11

Corralie closed her eyes as Ellen brushed her hair.

"Oh, Ellen, it's so good to be home again."

The last rays of the evening sun fell across the opened pot-pourri jar, releasing the gentle scent of cypress rose into the boudoir. Through the window she could see the rolling parkland and the ornamental fountains and waterfalls that were her father's pride and joy. The water seemed so clear and sparkling after the morning's storm, and the countless cultivated ferns clustering the sides of the pools looked as if washed and rejuvenated. In the distance, where the land dropped, she could see the sparkle of the sunset on the sea. Selney Bill crept out into the gathering dusk, hazy and indistinct, and beyond that, invisible from the Somerfords' great house, was Chacehampton Bay. She leaned back as Ellen's soothing hands brushed on and on. The thick, almost jungle-like foliage of Bottom Wood lined the far end of the park, and although she could not see, she knew that the *Laura* rocked in her safe anchorage on the river. High tide or low tide, the deepened mooring was full, although the cutter could only leave at high tide to cross the shoal water by the river's mouth. She pondered, not for the first time, what would happen if the Revenue men ever did find that hiding place. Would they believe her father's protestations of ignorance? She smiled at the thought, for as always, if enough money passed hands, his pleas would be accepted; and money was one thing her father possessed in plenty.

"Miss Corralie, what was Lady Catherine's maid like?" Ellen's earnest little face looked at her in the oval mirror.

"Not as excellent as you, Ellen."

"She's French, isn't she?"

"Yes."

"She'd done your hair up nice." The admission came grudgingly.

"She was good."

"Do you want your hair all Frenchified then, Miss Corralie?"

"No—it takes too long to dress. Besides, I think I look just as well *à l'Anglais,* don't you?"

"Oh, *yes,* Miss Corralie. There now, it's shining just nicely, but I think I should mix up a new rinse for tomorrow. A vinegar rinse. Which flowers should I steep in it overnight?"

"Oh, I cannot think. Lavender and rosebuds, I think. Yes, that will do nicely."

"I've put your letter on your pillow, Miss Corralie."

"Letter?"

The maid smiled, blushing and patting her brown curls into place self-consciously. "It's from that Captain Richardson—his name's on the back."

"It was *you* who had the fancy for the good captain, not me."

"He was ever so handsome in his uniform, wasn't he, Miss Corralie?"

"I suppose so, but I'd warrant young Danny Juro wouldn't think so if he could see your face now."

"Danny doesn't mean anything to me."

"Fibber. Go on—you've been angling for him since I don't know when."

Ellen's blush deepened. "That was before I went to London with you."

"And seem to have got ideas above your station! A captain of the hussars indeed, whatever next!"

"I only said he was handsome." Ellen cleaned Corralie's hairbrush. "Danny's got to be Hobby this year on Five Warriors' Night."

"Has he? Oh, that *is* an honor, isn't it? A man can only be Hobby once, is that not so?"

"Yes, Miss Corralie. I've got the costume to stitch up ready—it had some tears in it from last year."

"I'm not surprised. As I recall, last year's festivities got a little out of hand one way or another."

Ellen laughed. "Shall you write back to Captain Richardson, miss?"

"No."

"Go on, Miss Corralie. It'd take your mind off ——Oh, begging your pardon." Ellen went red and bit her lip.

"Off Lord Kendal? I doubt that the captain is in the same league."

"Give him a chance."

"I wasn't that impressed with him—far too much the dandy for me."

Ellen fluffed back the coverlets of the blue damask bed and the smell of lavender rose from the crisp sheets. "He was just perfect. Just perfect. Oh, go on, Miss Corralie, if only to spite *her*—just to let her know as you don't care two penny figs."

"To spite who?"

"Miss Fancy-Nose Tindling, the smuggler's daughter with notions above herself."

"Ellen, that will be enough. When she marries Lord Kendal, she will be *Lady* Kendal and you must speak of her with respect."

"Going to lah-de-dah schools and having grand wardrobes don't make her a proper lady. I've known her too long to be fooled. She's playing him double already."

Corralie paused in the tying of her nightdress ribbons. "What do you mean by that?"

"I shouldn't have said anything."

"I know that, but now that you have begun, pray go on and finish the tidbit."

"It's just gossip, Miss Corralie. She's been seen meeting someone else, someone who don't have no limp or walking cane." Ellen nervously fluffed the coverlet again. "That's all I've heard."

"And how certain is this gossip?"

"My sister told me. Her youngest said he saw them."

"Doing what?"

Ellen flushed. "Kissing. Leastways, he thinks that's what he saw, but he wasn't that close. Any road, she was meeting someone secretly."

"And this man Averil was meeting, who is he?"

"Jakey couldn't see him. He only knew it was Miss Nose-in-the-Air on account of her dogcart. Oh, there's Mr. Somerford coming up for his nightcap with you. Good evening, Mr. Somerford." Ellen bobbed a curtsey.

"Evening to you, Ellen. Run along, there's a good gel, and put plenty of brandy in it, eh? Can't abide insipid brown betty."

"Yes, Mr. Somerford."

Reynold drew a chair beside the little fire that flickered in the fireplace, poking at the pot-pourri jar with his slippered foot. "Cypress rose again?"

"I like it best."

"Prefer sandalwood and cinnamon myself."

She smiled fondly at him. "That is because Lady Agnes told you that as a Virgoan you must like sandalwood, and as having been born on a Wednesday you must also like cinnamon."

"Like the combination anyway," he grunted, grinning sheepishly. "Damned admirable woman, Lady Agnes."

"Make an honest woman of her, then."

"*Marry* her?"

"Why not? You could have blissful arguments all night and all day to your hearts' content."

"We *don't* argument constantly!"

"Father!"

Ellen brought in two cups of steaming brown betty and placed them on the little gilt table by the fire.

Corralie nodded at her. "That will be all then, Ellen. Good night."

"Good night, Miss Corralie. Mr. Somerford."

"Night to you, Ellen."

He picked up his cup and sniffed it appreciatively. "I look forward to my nightcap—she's got a gift for preparing this, that maid of yours."

"Father—about Bracken."

"Ah yes, well, the brute's gone. Back where it damn well came from."

"You would not fib to me?"

"It's the truth, woman, that I promise you." He smiled at her. "There's a surprise for you in the stables when you go there in the morning."

"A surprise? A new horse?"

"Wait and see."

"Please tell me."

"No. Now drink up your nightcap. How was Agnes's niece when last you saw her?"

"Catti? Not very well really, I think." Corralie looked from the window at the last rays of the sun on the sea. "What do you know of Sir Madoc Vaughan?"

"Know? That he was in the Foreign Office until recently. That he is not the most wealthy of gentlemen. That his reputation in London caused a good deal of fluttering and vapors among the fair sex. That is about all."

"And Catti's husband, Charles Beauchamp?"

"Nothing, nothing at all."

"I think he's a cavalry officer."

"Still don't mean anything to me, I'm afraid. Why?"

"Curiosity." She smiled. Perhaps she should say something to her father, something about the strange French lugger and about the damage to the *Fair Maid*, but somehow——

"There's not much love lost between Lawrence and Vaughan, is there?" said Reynold suddenly. "Can't for the life of me think why. Vaughan's done nothing that I know of to upset Lawrence. You know of anything?"

She felt uncomfortable. "Not really."

"That means you do."

"No, I don't."

Reynold studied her, sipping thoughtfully at his drink. "Vaughan been showing an interest in you, has he? That would make Lawrence grit his teeth."

"Don't be silly."

"It's not silly. The damned fool might have chosen Tindling's daughter, but he'd like to have you as well. I know him well enough to know that by now. Dog in the manger."

"Lawrence isn't like that."

"Isn't he? You think about it. Well, that's my drink done with and I have to be up in the early hours."

"At the observatory?"

"Sky's interesting at the moment. Oh, by the

way—I'd almost forgotten to tell you—I've invited old Chadders to dine with us on the evening of the first. Put up with him, eh Corry? For my sake?"

"Of course I will. I'll smile sweetly and be gone as promptly as humanly possible from the dining table." She smiled. "*I* have a dinner invitation, too."

"Who from?"

"Lawrence."

"Just you?"

"Good heavens, no! Lawrence, Averil, myself, and Sir Madoc."

Reynold grinned. "Lawrence *is* churning around, isn't he? Well, good night to you, my dear."

"Good night, Father."

He went to the door and then nodded at the window. "Harry's working on the *Laura* tonight—there'll be cognac again for us soon. With luck."

"If you didn't guzzle it so, you would not be needing so much of it."

"I don't guzzle—I savor. Good night, m'dear."

"Good night."

It was almost midnight. Lawrence leaned back against the *Fair Maid*'s mast and watched the Tindling house. Shadows moved against the chintz curtains of the little kitchen. He lit a thin cigar and inhaled it thoughtfully.

The door opened and two figures were silhouetted against the light of the oil lamps inside. The man kissed Averil's hand, holding it as he spoke; and then he drew her closer and kissed her on the lips. Lawrence dropped the half-smoked cigar and stamped it out. The man had gone now, melting between the crowded buildings on the quayside. The lights in the house were extinguished.

Lawrence leaned his head wearily back against the mast and stared up at the idle rigging. The mast rocked gently on the tide, swaying across the starry heavens with a soothing motion. So much for the cousin from Abbotsworth. "Oh, Averil, Averil——" he murmured.

The dip-dip of oars made him turn his head, and he watched the *Laura*'s longboat slide smoothly past the cutter. Harry's burly figure sat in the stern, his flat-crowned hat with its wide brim hiding his bearded face. He would return to find only his daughter in the house. Lawrence remained motionless as the longboat slipped away astern, vanishing around the quay and into the boatyard.

12

Wearing her pale green woolen riding habit, Corralie hurried into the stable yard.

"Gerry?"

The groom ducked beneath a rail and grinned at her. "Morning, Miss Corralie. In the end stall back there."

As Corralie's shadow fell across the stall, the dun mare turned her graceful head and pricked her ears.

"Pippit!"

Gerry came to stand next to her. "Ah—a powerful good-looking mare, is that one an' all."

"But how did she come here?"

"Sir Madoc brought her over last evening. Said as she was for you and wouldn't hear no no's. Insisted. Said it was a gift."

"But I can't accept a gift like that!" Corralie patted the mare's glossy neck.

Gerry shrugged. "Reckon you'll have a job giving her back, then. He was powerful determined to give her to you."

"Have her tacked up for me, will you?"

"She's a sight skittish, mind."

"I know, I've ridden her before."

When the mare was ready, Gerry helped her into the sidesaddle. "Gerry, will you send word into the house that I've ridden over to Webley?"

"Yes, Miss Corralie."

She rode across the lawns toward the lodge, smiling and nodding at the lodgekeeper as he opened the wrought-iron gates for her. The lane smelled of hawthorn as Pippit cantered toward the town, and the sun shone warmly over the countryside. The seagulls were high, wheeling and crying over the beach beyond the trees of Bottom Wood, and the mellow sound of St. James's bell sounded as she rode into Chacehampton. On impulse, she decided to ride along the quayside, for it was one of her favorite spots. The *Fair Maid* was deserted as Corralie passed, and the fishing boats were just leaving the harbor, rising on each swelling wave as it surged down the narrow harbor entrance.

Corralie reined in suddenly as a figure in primrose muslin stepped from Miss Yelverton's dressmaking establishment.

"Good morning, Averil."

"Good morning, Corralie, how good it is to see you again." The polite words were empty. Averil's eyes went to Pippit and her parasol twirled busily. "Is that not——?"

"Yes, it is."

"You persuaded him after all?"

"In a manner of speaking—He has given her to me."

The parasol twirled more vigorously. "*Given* her?"

"I was riding to see him now."

The parasol stopped abruptly. "How fortunate you are, Corralie."

Corralie glanced at the model in the dressmaker's

bow window. "You have been for a fitting of your wedding gown?"

"Yes."

"How fortunate *you* are."

Averil looked at her and then smiled faintly. "Perhaps." The parasol twirled again, causing the fluffy feathers in her bonnet to stir. "You will never approve of me, will you, Corralie?"

"It has nothing to do with me, Averil."

"Hasn't it? I tell you this, if you try to do any-thing, *any*thing, I will turn him from you once and for all. I can do it, you know." The cool, gray eyes were steady.

"I don't want to be at odds with you, Averil, and I have done nothing to warrant the threat you just made. I acknowledge defeat and accept that you are to marry him. I am prepared to let it rest at that. I will be harmless in the future, I do assure you. And now, I will bid you good morning."

Corralie kicked her heel and Pippit moved away down the quay, turning into the narrow street where St. James's Church stood on the corner.

Averil watched her and then turned her gaze toward Webley, so far across the bay. Tears filled her eyes and she bowed her head, walking hur-riedly along the busy quay toward the boatyard.

Corralie rode through the lanes toward Webley, enjoying the warmth of the sun and determined to shake off the gloom that Averil had managed to in-voke. Dog roses sprawled over the crumbling walls of a ruined cottage, creeping carelessly through the gaping windows and over the once-blue porch. The wild honeysuckle was out in the hedgerows and everywhere there were heavy white boughs of hawthorn. The gloom was evaporating as she reached the crossroads, and her daydreaming al-most caused the accident.

Madoc was forced to rein in the curricle's fast-trotting team, and Catti squealed as she grabbed at the rail. "Corralie!"

Pippit reared and snorted, but Corralie had control enough to calm the frightened horse. She slipped from the saddle and went to stroke Pippit's velvety nose, smiling at Madoc.

"It seems that I am destined to fall at your feet whenever we meet."

He handed the ribbons to Catti and climbed down from the high perch. "And you also seem determined to stop my heart, one way or another." He smiled at her.

"I was coming to see you," she said.

"My cup runneth over."

"About Pippit."

"Ah. Surely you are not about to refuse my well-intentioned offering?"

She shook her head. "I should grumble and protest, but I cannot—I want her too much."

"That is at least honest, for which I thank you."

"*Thank* me? Why?" she asked.

He pulled one of Pippit's ears. "For paying me the compliment of saying exactly what you mean—it is an all too common failing these days when folk say anything and everything but what they actually mean."

"Riddles."

"I know you understand me, Corralie."

She looked at him and then nodded. "I know. And thank you again." She turned to Catti. "Are you well, Catti?"

"Well enough, Corralie—especially as I have at last persuaded my brother to take me for that drive."

"Have you further news of your husband?"

Catti's lips parted and she glanced at Madoc. "No—no more news."

Madoc removed his hat and hung it over the saddle. "You have been talking of Charles?"

Corralie smiled at him. "I found her so low one morning, and she said that she had had word he would not be coming for another month."

He smiled in return, but she could sense the wariness in his interest. "Such is the way of army service, it is not?" he murmured.

"Yes. Lawrence never knew if his orders would be changed at the last minute."

Catti toyed with her tapestry reticule for a moment and then looked at Corralie. "Shall you take luncheon with us at Webley, Corralie? Oh, I *would* like that! Aunt Agnes is visiting friends and there is only myself and Madoc. Do join us."

Madoc nodded. "Yes, I second that invitation."

"I would like that very much." Corralie was very conscious of him as he leaned to take up his top hat, and she turned to mount Pippit again. He lifted her lightly onto the saddle and handed her the reins.

"If I promise, Corralie, to drive very very slowly and carefully, will you promise not to send my heart into my mouth again?"

She smiled. "I will do my very best, and sit like a limpet on a rock."

The surf hissed over the shining pebbles of Webley Bay and Catti sighed contentedly, leaning back against the rock. "I think Aunt Agnes would have the vapors if she knew we'd come down here to eat."

Corralie smiled. "I doubt it very much. She and my father once sat all night in his observatory waiting for one particular star or planet to appear, and between them they consumed two bottles of Burgundy, a loaf of bread, two pounds of blue vinney, and half a seed cake. I'll warrant the good busybodies of Chacehampton would give their eyeteeth to have such a juicy tidbit to buzz over town."

Catti laughed and settled further back against the rock, closing her eyes. "I'm so sleepy now, after that cold chicken salad and chilled hock. Warm sunshine, sea air, and good company." She smiled without opening her eyes. "I can almost forget——" She didn't finish the sentence.

Madoc loosened his flapping cravat and looked around the bay, his hair blowing across his face. "Warm sunshine, sea air, and good company. There is much to be said for Dorset, Corralie." He smiled at her.

"One cannot even *like* London after living here."

"Not even the endless balls, the salons, and drawing-room intrigue?"

"No."

"And no one in your life apart from Kendal."

She flushed. "How did you know?" Her eyes went to Catti.

"Catti told me nothing. You told me yourself— you murmur most interestingly when half-conscious."

She looked away. "I don't want to talk about it."

"In Kendal's shoes I wouldn't have chosen Averil Tindling."

"But you are *not* Lawrence."

He smiled. "No, I am infinitely preferable."

"Are Librans noted for swollen-headedness, too?" she asked, looking again at Catti's sleeping face.

"My sister is sleeping soundly enough not to hear what we say," he said, ignoring her question. He leaned back and looked up at the cloudless sky. "She lies awake at nights, worrying and yearning— thank God she sleeps now."

Corralie thought of the tap-tapping dancing from

the room where Charles Beauchamp's portrait hung. "Why hasn't he come back, Madoc?"

His eyes swung to her face. "I wish that I knew."

The words struggled on her lips, and she was on the point of blurting what she knew, but suddenly Catti awoke with a start.

"Oh Lord, I dreamed I was falling!"

Madoc smiled at her. "Your head was rolling, that's all."

"It gave me such a startling." She got to her feet. "Do you know, I think I could go to my bed and sleep really well."

Madoc stood and kissed her. "Do that then, Catti, and get rid of those shadows beneath your eyes. Charles will not recognize you, will he? Mm?"

She smiled at Corralic. "Would you be very miffed at me if I left you after being the one to invite you here?"

"No. It's time I took myself home, anyway, or my father will be sending out search parties. He's been like that ever since Sir John Tilley's daughter was kidnapped and ransomed."

Madoc laughed. "One of the perils of being rich! I will ride back with you and make certain of your safe return."

"Oh, there is no need——"

"I want to—if you'll have me." He pointed up at Bascombe Heath. "We can go that way, even if there *is* no rain today."

She smiled.

13

The view from the Five Warriors was magnificent on so fine a day. Madoc climbed onto the fallen stone and stood there, looking down at Webley Bay.

"I had not realized my aunt's bay was so visible from up here."

"Why, have you taken to bathing?" she asked with a laugh.

But for once he did not respond to the humor. He stared down at the little curve of the bay, snatching his cravat from around his neck and pushing it into his pocket. "I gather there is some sort of ceremony up here soon?"

"Yes."

"When?"

"The first full moon of June." *Full moon.* Corralie glanced swiftly down at the bay. That was when——

"What happens?"

"Oh, everyone in Chacehampton comes up here, leading a man dressed up as the king, and they all make as much noise as they possibly can, leading the king around and around the Warriors. When he gets tired, they sit down and have some refreshments, and then they begin again. Until the moon cannot be seen in the sky anymore, and then they all retire to their beds."

Madoc stared at her. "Whatever is it in aid of?"

"When you look so taken aback at our country junketings, I do not know that I shall tell you."

He smiled. "What is it about, Corralie?"

"Well, hundreds of years ago there was a battle, and the enemy came ashore down at Chacehampton. The local king was defeated and with his only five remaining warriors, he came up here to the heath. The enemy began to pursue them and the king lost his nerve, fleeing back down to join the enemy, and the five warriors were so disgraced by their monarch's behavior, that they turned to stone."

Madoc sat down and leaned back on one elbow. "I wonder there are not more blocks of stone at Carlton House, then."

"That is unkind."

"What is behind all these goings-on with a mock king?"

"The original battle happened on a full-moon night, and the reason for the battle going against the king was that the local people fought on the side of the enemy. So, once a year, on full moon in June, they have to bring the king back up and drum him around his five warriors and so prevent them from coming to life and going down to wreak their terrible vengeance upon the townsfolk."

He laughed. "And it is all a grand excuse for getting drunk."

"We don't all get drunk."

"*You* join in? I am astounded."

"Don't be so superior—it's a most enjoyable evening."

He looked down at the bay again. "Bascombe Heath is crowded then on the next full moon."

"Yes."

He turned to look over toward Selney Bill. The *Janus* was still at anchor in the sheltered lee of the promontory, and even as they looked, the light flashed from the old fortifications. Neither Corralie nor Madoc said anything, but turned to stare at the horizon. After two or three minutes a ship appeared.

"A ketch," he said.

"They signal to the *Janus* when they see anything that can't be seen either from the sloop or from anywhere else nearby on land."

"How do you know?"

"Lawrence noticed."

"Our hawk-eyed sea lordling?"

She flushed. "Don't speak of him like that. Why don't you like him?"

"Because he doesn't like me—I am most observant, you note."

"He thinks you are about to pursue me for my money." She watched his face carefully for any reaction.

"That does not take a genius to work out."

"Thank you very much, Madoc Vaughan!"

"Ah—but I would pursue you anyway, because I want you."

"Madoc, if I were a mere serving girl, I would not see your excellently clad heels for dust!"

"If you were a serving girl, I would not be wasting my time sitting here chitter-chattering, I would be proving to you how enjoyable an armful I can be when the mood takes me."

"I can believe that."

He climbed down. "What? That I could be proving myself? Or that I would be enjoyable?"

This conversation was moving too swiftly—— She looked at him. "Both. Probably."

He put his hand against her neck, his fingers moving in her dark red hair. "Only the wondrous thought of your fortune protects you now from my most base instincts, but as recompense I will accept a mere kiss as payment for Pippit."

"I thought her to be a gift." Her voice was husky and her pulses were racing.

"Then a kiss of thanks will do as well. Corralie."

She stared at him. *A fortune-hunting adventurer he may be, but*—— She did not resist as he kissed her, and when he put his arms around her she held him.

He brushed his lips against her eyelids. "I enjoy being with you far too much for my blasted sanity," he said at last.

She drew away. "I want to believe that, Madoc."

"Then believe it."

She smiled. "I cannot—I look into your wicked Welsh eyes and feel for certain that I am being duped."

"I am cut to the quick."

"You are master of your art, Madoc."

"And therefore not to be believed?"

"And therefore to be viewed warily."

He smiled. "Hoist with my own petard? Ah well, *c'est la vie.*"

"It's getting late, I must be going."

"Corralie—I *did* mean what I said."

She turned to look at him again. "And so did I. I do want to believe you."

"But?"

"But."

He nodded. "Let us leave it, then. For the moment."

"I will ride on by myself, Madoc. Your presence confuses me."

He lifted her onto Pippit's saddle and then took her hand, turning the palm to his lips. "I shall convince you in the end."

"When you begin to tell me the truth about things, then I shall listen to you, Madoc Vaughan."

"The truth?"

But she had gone, urging Pippit away from the standing stones and across the heath. He stood there, toying with The Beau's reins, and then he mounted and turned back toward Webley.

14

Corralie glanced at her fobwatch. There were two hours yet before Captain Chadwick and his officers arrived. She sighed inwardly; the Captain on his own was bad enough, but the prospect of his officers as well was rather paralyzing. If she had known in time that her father had recklessly invited so many, she would have begged Lady Agnes to come to her aid, but now it was too late and she must be the only lady present. *I shall be like a queen bee.*

She followed the butler across the black-and-white tiled vestibule and waited as he threw open the gold and white double doors of the dining room.

The maids fidgeted in a neat row, looking very crisp and clean in their gray seersucker dresses, white aprons, and mobcaps. The footmen were more elegant in their powdered periwigs, charcoal coats, and gold braiding. The butler cleared his throat.

"If you will inspect everything, Miss Corralie."

She walked the length of the polished mahogany table, with its silver cutlery and low bowls of dark red roses. The cut crystal glasses sparkled in the light of the shimmering chandeliers, and pools of warm light were thrown over the new crimson silk wallpaper. Corralie looked at the walls with a certain smug satisfaction, for she and her father had long argued about the color. He was so conservative at times, always wanting something restrained and almost muted. But this, her one burst of extravagance, was surely perfect for this elegant room with its tall row of windows overlooking the ornamental pools and fountains.

"It looks excellent, Haines, in fact it looks very good indeed. Perfect. Now, the food. Are there enough pineapples in the hothouse?"

"Yes, Miss Corralie, but I have had to send Gerry to Dorchester to see if Mister Kent has any peaches—I fear the mildew has spoiled ours this year."

"He is not back yet?"

"Not yet."

"Oh well, the navy will have to be content with pineapples, grapes, and strawberries. Has the epergne been repaired properly this time? I don't want a repetition of that catastrophe at Christmas when two bowls fell from it and dislodged the cheese board. Drunken members of the local hunt pursuing escaped Edam cheeses is not my notion of at capital evening."

The butler smiled. "The goldsmith in Dorchester saw to it last week, Miss Corralie, and it's being prepared down in the kitchens now. When last I saw it a few minutes ago, it was looking most splendid."

"No doubt it does, Haines. Now, is there anything else I should ask about? My mind somehow will not seem to work properly for me tonight."

"Well, I sent a man to the icehouse this afternoon with a pony and he brought back more than enough for the champagne and white wine."

"The coffee?"

"From London on yesterday's mail, Miss Corralie."

"The liqueurs?"

"All in hand, Miss Corralie."

"That reminds me, Haines, you are to rescue me with some excuse directly the liqueurs are served."

He nodded. "I shall discover some suitable mishap in the kitchens that requires your attention, Miss Corralie."

"At least I shall be spared the more boisterous chit-chat, then." *And Captain Chadwick's disapproving stares and grumbles——*

She glanced around the room again and nodded. "It all looks just as I like it, Haines. Thank you. You may, of course, take four bottles from the cellar as usual for yourselves, and taste anything you choose from the dishes that go back to the kitchens."

"Thank you, Miss Corralie."

She began to leave and then turned suddenly. "The finger bowls!"

The butler's mouth dropped. "I had forgotten them!"

"And has someone been sent to the observatory to bring my father down? Otherwise he'll forget his guests and stay there all night."

"Someone was sent a short while ago, Miss Corralie."

"Then I think everything is in hand and I may take myself to my rooms to dress."

"All is going excellently, Miss Corralie."

The evening was cooler than she had expected and the flimsy Indian gauze gown did not afford much warmth. The silver embroidery on the dainty mauve cloth shone as she sat forward to hear what Captain Chadwick had to say.

" 'Pon me soul, dashed good champagne. Dry as a whore's——Begging your pardon, a slip of the tongue."

She smiled wearily. The Captain was no doubt a splendid officer and the backbone of England at times of war, but at the dinner table he was the absolute and utter end. When he walked, he strode as if the world was the deck of the *Janus* and he always spoke in short sharp bursts, like gunfire.

"My father prides himself on his cellar, Captain Chadwick."

"Always did like his beverages."

"You've known each other a long time?"

"Since school. Then the fool went and got himself wed."

"You have never married, Captain?"

He scowled, his graying whiskers reacting almost as a cat's hackles would. "Good God, no!"

His loud exclamation ended the other more muted conversations and everyone turned to look.

Chadwick did not seem to notice, for he helped himself to more champagne without bothering to even glance at Corralie's glass. "Can't abide women—damned fool squealing and chattering. Man can't think."

"No doubt." She threw a heartfelt glance at her father, who chose to deliberately look the other way. She decided to try again, however, smiling sweetly at the unpleasant captain. "And what brings you to Chacehampton, Captain Chadwick?"

"Damned Admiralty telegraph, that's what!"

"I beg your pardon?"

"Blasted clacking thing. Twelve minutes on a good day—orders from Admiralty to Portsmouth. Blasted sun shone like a beacon, didn't it? Another few minutes and I'd have been over the horizon and on me way to Boney."

"I don't understand."

The captain glowered. *Women.* "The Admiralty telegraph—it takes only minutes to transmit orders from London. I was already on my way in the *Janus* to the Mediterranean. Elba. But the telegraph brought new orders and the pilot followed me offshore and delivered the new orders. Is that clearer?"

"Yes." She mentally gritted her teeth, for he had spoken as slowly as if to a three-year-old. "And why were you diverted to Chacehampton, of all places?"

"Classified."

With some degree of relief she saw Haines carrying in the coffeepot. Salvation would shortly come her way.

The young first lieutenant on her other side leaned closer, smiling. "*I* promise not to bite your head off, Miss Somerford."

"I have no head left, I fancy."

"Oh, but you have, and most exquisite it is, too."

She smiled at him. "Are all first lieutenants so charming?"

"We try."

"Tell me, is there really a telegraph from the Admiralty to Portsmouth?"

"Oh yes. It flashes a series of signals from high vantage point to high vantage and thence into the dockyard. As Captain Chadwick said, on a sunny day the messages can travel the whole distance in only twelve minutes."

"I am most impressed."

"Captain Chadwick wasn't—he was dashed furious when the *Janus* was turned back. He was looking forward to Elba." He leaned closer and dropped his voice. "Visions of recapturing the Em-

peror should he break out of his new little empire,
I fancy."

She laughed. "A grand prize indeed for a mere
sloop."

"Aye, today the *Janus*, tomorrow First Lord."

She laughed again, liking him. He was in his
early thirties, a rugged man with soft brown hair
and hazel eyes. "You are married, Mister Hughes?"

"No, indeed, but betrothed."

"And where is your fiancée?"

"Cheltenham—with her parents. We hope to
marry this coming autumn."

"I wish you happiness then, Mister Hughes." She
raised her glass.

"Thank you, Miss Somerford. But then, surely,
you are not unattached?" His eyes moved over her
with appreciation. "If you are, then it must be because you nurse a broken heart."

She flushed. "I am not sure anymore—and that,
sir, is the truth."

"Happiness, Miss Somerford, is never a thing one
is *unsure* about. Take it when it appears."

She looked at him. "Perhaps you are right—but
then it is not always so simple, is it?"

"Not always. But one would imagine anything
and everything would be simple and clear here in
Chacehampton."

"Why? Because it is so sleepy and dreamy a
township?"

"Ah—well, that is not what I have heard about
it."

"What have you heard, then?"

"That the folk hereabouts are the biggest set of
scoundrels this side of Tyburn."

"Good heavens, are we really? Is that why the
Janus is here?"

He sat back. "In a way—and I've said far too

much already. I have little desire to be flogged around the fleet."

"Your crime would hardly warrant so drastic a punishment."

"Idle chatter and carelessness with secrecy is quite a crime, Miss Somerford."

"Then I have not heard a thing you have said to me so far this evening, Mister Hughes."

She felt suddenly that the presence of the *Laura* beyond the trees of Bottom Wood was almost sensed by the young lieutenant who smiled so charmingly at her. An uncomfortable color stole over her face. Unless, of course—it was not on account of Harry Tindling that the *Janus* was here. What if it was because of Madoc Vaughan's brother-in-law? But the uncomfortable color did not go with this thought, which was somehow not reassuring in the slightest. A finger of fear touched her spine as she looked around at the smiling faces of the officers. And it was fear for Madoc. Were they all in Chacehampton because of him? She touched the little silver spoon beside her coffee, pushing it gently around the porcelain saucer. *I will have to tell him what I know*——

"Miss Corralie?"

She started as the butler spoke close by.

"Miss Corralie, I am afraid that there is a slight problem in the kitchens that requires your attention."

"Oh. Oh, yes. Of course. If you will excuse me, gentlemen. Please have the liqueurs served, Haines. I shall not disturb you again, gentlemen, and so I bid you good night."

Murmuring politely and scraping their chairs as they stood, they bowed to her. She smiled at the lieutenant. "I hope indeed that you marry your lady from Cheltenham in the autumn, Mister Hughes."

He kissed her hand. "I think that our business here will be well finished by then, Miss Somerford."

The cold finger ran up her spine again as she inclined her head and left the dining room.

15

Reynold folded the *Times* and put away his spectacles. "There will come a day when I can receive the London papers on the day they are published—you mark my words."

She smiled. "You will needs must train an extremely large and vigorous pigeon, Father."

He took the lid from his glass of camomile tea and sipped it, replacing the lid immediately and grimacing. "Oh, my head——"

"If you will insist upon playing foolish games of war on the front lawns in the early hours of the morning with Chadders and his officers, then you deserve to have a headache."

"Unfeeling wench."

"What time *did* you all part company?"

"Four this morning."

"Shame on you."

He put the cold, damp cloth against his forehead again and leaned back in the armchair. "You are tetchy this morning, Corry—tetchy and definitely unsympathetic!"

"I did not sleep well."

"We were not *that* rowdy, Corry," he protested, wincing as he raised his voice slightly.

"Oh, it wasn't your junketings that kept me awake." She pushed a wayward curl beneath her mobcab, but it immediately fell out again.

"Leave your hair alone, girl, and tell me what's wrong. I cannot abide moods."

"I am not in a mood."

"What is it, then? Eh? Mooning over Lawrence still?"

"No!"

"Vaughan, then—it must be one or the other."

"I *do* have wider interests, Father."

"Maybe—but in this instance it has to be Lawrence or Madoc Vaughan. In a dither are you?"

She looked away. "Why do you say that?"

"Because you've always been wearing your heart on your sleeve for Lawrence. *Always.* But now, suddenly, Vaughan appears—and he obviously is making interested noises, to say the least. Witness the gift of that thoroughbred mare—she's blue-blooded, *dark* blue. And you, my girl, are not impervious to his undoubted charm, are you? Mm?"

"No."

"Well, at least it makes a change from the hopeless yearnings for Lawrence. But mark my words, you had better tread carefully with Vaughan, for it's *my* money you'll be inheriting, and I don't want it bestowed upon someone who's simply after your wealth and not you yourself. Corry?"

"Yes?"

"Were you paying attention to what I said?"

"Yes. Oh, Father, do you think I have not been thinking about just that for most of my adult life? I *know* that it is not my beauty and vivacity that draw the interest, but my future prospects."

"Oh, my poor Corry."

She stood and went to the window, determined to change the subject. "Father, what uniform is it that's navy blue all over, with gold crusting on the coat and dark red cuffs and facings? And a pelisse trimmed with black fur?"

He stared thoughtfully at the portrait of his grandfather on the wall above the ornate fireplace. "*Gold* braiding, you say?"

"Yes."

"I was about to say the Tenth Hussars, but their braiding is silver and their pelisses trimmed with white fur. I don't think I know—why do you ask?"

"Oh, I saw a portrait——"

"Tell you what, bring that journal that Polish fellow gave me, the folder thing with all the loose pages inside. Yes, that's the one. Give it here and we'll have a look through. That Pole was a genius, a veritable genius—see? More perfect drawings and paintings of uniforms than you'll find anywhere." He opened it carefully, forgetting his aching head and delicate stomach as he looked at each sheet of paper. "Now then—a hussar uniform, dark blue with gold braiding."

They slowly went through the folder, gazing at the delicately painted drawings. "Well, it's not here, Corry, unless—— Well, there's that one." He pulled out a sheet and held it up.

She stared at the water color. It was the same, even down to the leopardskin shabrack on the horse. It was the identical uniform. "I'm sure that's it, Father. What regiment is it?"

"Whose portrait was it, Corry?"

"I—I don't know, it was just a portrait. I rather admired the uniform, that's all." She did not want to tell him, although why, she could not have said. "Why?"

"Why? Because it's French. Aide-de-camp to a

Marshal of the Imperial Army, no less. An exalted *parlez-vous*."

"Are you sure?"

"Damn it, Corry—if you won't take my word for it then read what's been written underneath. See?"

She read the penciled writing and then put the painting back in the folder. It was true—Charles Beauchamp was wearing one of Bonaparte's uniforms. Could it be that he was not Charles Beauchamp the Englishman, but *Charles Beauchamp* the Frenchman?

"Where'd you see it, Corry?"

"Oh—in London somewhere."

He looked at her for a long moment and then nodded. "A handsome enough get-up—typical French peacockry. Boney's notion of uniforms only just stops short of the ridiculous sometimes."

She closed the folder and took it back to its drawer in the escritoire. Reynold watched her and said nothing more. He sipped some more camomile tea. "Harry's cutter's almost ship-shape again—he stopped here this morning before you came down. I—er, advised him to shift the *Laura* as soon as he could."

"Why?"

"Something Chadders said last night. I think the old dog's remembered that river anchorage—from way back when he stayed here once. Anyway, Harry's playing safe and getting her out. By the way, he said he's got some really top-drawer Brussels lace at his house. He thought you'd be interested."

"Doesn't dear Averil want it, then?"

"Apparently not."

"Neither do I. If I wore it, she'd recognize it and feel damned superior. I wouldn't give the bitch the chance."

Reynold raised his eyebrows. "You're still tetchy, my dear."

Madoc led Catti into the garden, not saying anything until they were well away from the gardeners.

"I have to go to London for a day or so, Catti."

"Why? There's nothing wrong?"

"No, sister mine, there's nothing wrong. I do have affairs of my own to attend to, you know. Like the sale of my other house to meet my debts."

"Not Ethrington Street."

"Yes. I could not sell Webley over Aunt Agnes' head, now, could I?"

"Faro was your downfall, Madoc Vaughan—that and maraschino punch at the Duchess's party."

"One drunken, exhilarating night certainly put paid to my fortunes." He smiled. "When this business is over, perhaps I can begin to recoup my losses, eh?"

"Corralie, you mean?"

"She would be the answer to my most fervent prayers, yes."

"I like her, Madoc, and I wouldn't like her to be hurt by you."

"*Cariad*, I wouldn't hurt her—far from it, in fact. Far indeed. But I fancy all would be lost should she realize about myself and Averil."

"And that was on my account! Oh, Madoc!" Her eyes were full of self-blame.

He put his arm around her. "It cannot be helped, for your troubles are more important, aren't they?"

"Did—did you find out anything from Averil?"

"Tindling's cutter is almost ready to put to sea again."

"Oh, no——"

"The chances of his coming face to face with the *Belle Marie* are fairly slender, Catti."

"But there is still a chance."

"Yes, that I cannot deny. And he and Darnier hate each other's guts."

"And the *Laura* is heavily armed."

"Twenty-two cannon. We shall have to keep our fingers crossed." He smiled at her.

"And the sloop in Chacehampton? Do you know why she is here yet?"

"No. But Catti, it *can't* be because of the *Belle Marie*—no one could possibly know about her."

"They could—if something has gone wrong on Elba." She twisted her handkerchief anxiously. "Oh, would that I knew what was happening over there. Why wasn't he on the beach last time? *Why?*"

Madoc said nothing.

She smiled and hugged him. "Did ever a sister have a more loving and kind brother?"

"Never—the mold was broken after my creation." He dropped a kiss on her forehead. "Now then, I must be on my way to London if I am to be back for the fifth."

"What happens on the fifth that you are so intent upon getting back?"

"I dine at Kendal's."

"With Corralie?"

"Yes."

"I shall keep my fingers crossed for you, Madoc."

He smiled ruefully. "Catti, at any given time she could suddenly regain her memory of that accident. And if she does, she will remember who and what she saw in the depths of Bascombe Wood."

"Oh, Madoc——"

"Don't look at me like that. How else do you imagine I am able to wheedle information from Averil?"

"Well, it works, anyway."

"Oh, it works—it works marvelously. Except that she doesn't blasted well know where the *Laura* is berthed!"

She smiled ruefully. "It does have a funny side, you know."

"I know—but I'm damned if I particularly want to laugh."

16

The landau swayed along the lane toward Henarth, Lawrence's great mansion house on the Dorchester road. Corralie held up her hand looking glass again and looked at her hair. Ellen had spent so long over it with the curling iron, but it had been worth it, for the soft curls fell so beautifully from the jeweled comb at the back of her head. She moved her head slightly, and the perfume of lavender and roses drifted through the enclosed carriage. And each curl shone so. She stared at her face, at the touches of Portuguese rouge on her cheeks and lips, and the glittering earrings which felt so heavy.

She wore long, white evening gloves and a diamond bracelet that matched the earrings, and an evening gown of russet silk. She tied and untied the silver string, gathering it beneath her breasts, retying it in a more complicated bow, but still she could not feel satisfied. She looked well, she *knew* she did, but still she could not stop fidgeting.

She pulled her silver-threaded shawl around her shoulders and then toyed with the ties of her evening reticule.

The landau turned slowly through the great

phoenix-topped gates of Henarth and she heard
the coachman shouting down to the lodgekeeper.
Then there were servants carrying flambeaux running beside the carriage, their heavy footsteps au-
dible beyond the noise of the horses. Lanterns had
been strung in the trees, and the huge lake was
ringed with more lanterns, all in different colors
and shapes, their lights reflected in the darkening
water. The house itself was a blaze of color, the
windows all bright with lamps and candles and
chandeliers in the countless rooms, and as the landau swayed to a standstill, the perfume of pinks
filled the air. She stepped down and saw that the
steps of the house were strewn with pinks—Averil's
favorite flower.

She shook out her clinging skirts and looked
around. There was only one part of the gardens
close to the house where there was hardly any
light, and that was the maze that Lawrence's grandfather had planted in the middle of the last century.
Its high yew hedges looked impenetrable, and she
remembered how she and Lawrence had got lost
there on Lawrence's tenth birthday—and the wigging they both got for the trouble they had caused.

She ascended the flowery steps behind the footman and entered the gold and white entrance hall
with its magnificent ceiling painting of ancient
Egypt. Bowls of lotus flowers from the hothouse
stood on the low tables lining the walls, and the
floor was painted as if it were a pharaoh's water
garden with brilliantly plumed birds diving among
papyrus and greenery to catch silver fish in their
beaks.

She carefully stepped around each bird, as always she did, for fear of treading upon it, and followed the footman up the sapphire-carpeted steps
to the first-floor landing with its two Egyptian
mummies and curious statues of ebony-colored

pharaoh's, treasures brought back from Lawrence's boyhood visit to the land that had always captured his imagination. His father's death had seen the dressing-up of Henarth in as eccentric a fashion as any attention-seeking dandy in England could have desired.

As she neared the drawing room she heard the sound of Averil playing the harpsichord. Harry Tindling was an uncouth, rough man, but he had used his ill-gotten money well when he had sent his only child to a young ladies' school and had had her taught the ways of the rich.

Averil was a vision in pale pink gauze and silver lace. Her tawny hair was dressed in Grecian twists and ringlets and ornamented with a tiny posy of pinks. A ruby necklace glittered at her throat and on her finger was the engagement ring Lawrence had given her. The piece of music ended with a flourishing trill and she sat back, folding her hands demurely in her lap.

Lawrence clapped. "*Bravo*, Averil, I have seldom heard Mozart played more beautifully. Ah, there you are Corry. We began to think you were not coming." He smiled, holding out his hands to her.

"I am not late. Shame on you for hinting that I was."

Madoc stood, smiling at her. "Ah, Kendal, but the vision now presented to us was surely well worth any wait."

"Assuredly." Lawrence still held her hand, and led her toward the harpsichord, away from Madoc. "Shall you play for us again, Averil?"

"Perhaps Corralie does not want to hear my note-picking."

"Oh please, Averil, for you play so well." Corralie smiled as sweetly as she could, remembering the last exchange with the girl in pink gauze.

Averil began to play again, reveling in her superiority, and Corralie drew her hand from Lawrence's and turned to Madoc.

"Good evening, Madoc."

"Corralie."

"You returned from London in time, then?"

"By a short neck."

"Catti told me. You have sold your house?"

"I believe so." He smiled. "I have left it in the hands of my lawyers for the moment."

"I must talk with you tonight, Madoc."

"I look forward to that."

"I am troubled——" She wanted to say more, but Lawrence claimed her attention again, deliberately taking her back to the harpsichord where Averil's dextrous fingers were seemingly playing every note on the keyboard at the same time.

Oh, let her make a mess of it, please let her—— Corralie's uncharitable prayers were miraculously answered, for Averil went disastrously wrong and sat back, laughing to cover her confusion and humiliation.

Corralie turned to look at Madoc again, and he smiled at her.

The servants placed the extravagantly garnished round of veal on the table, surrounded by its entrées, and Corralie stared at it in dismay.

"Lawrence, we shall not be able to get up from the table afterward!"

"Corry, when you are invited to dine here, you may know that you will dine well."

Averil finished the last of her poached turbot in lobster sauce and sipped her Meursault. "I shall have to have my wedding gown let out by *inches!* What was that soup again? It was delicious."

"*Potage à la Monglas.*"

"And what was in it—that's what I really wanted

to know." She smiled at him, her eyes large and soft.

"Madeira, *foie gras,* truffles, and mushrooms."

She rolled her eyes at him. "So *fattening!* You will ruin my figure, Lawrence."

He smiled faintly, and not for the first time that evening Corralie noticed the slight reserve there when he spoke to Averil. He seemed withdrawn.

The footmen brought chilled dry champagne to accompany the veal, and Corralie nodded as another footman asked her if she would like some of the garnishing. As she nodded, she encountered a glance passing between Averil and Madoc. It was not much of a glance, a mere meeting of the eyes almost, and yet it caught Corralie's attention completely for a moment.

She looked away at Lawrence. "This feast must be a world away from the fare you had in the army."

"Eons away. Stewed ration-beef and paltry vegetables if we were lucky. I remember with shame the way we set about any partridge or hare we managed to snare—hardly drawing-room manners." He smiled at her. "Spain in the winter does not offer a great variety of anything much."

Madoc sampled the champagne. "But it offered glory, did it not?"

"Glory? Sometimes. Moments like an advance when we were so eager to get at the French that O'Callaghan had to shout *'Steady, Thirty-ninth! Ordinary time!'* Or when we captured the French eagle. Those are glories, are they not? It is easy to forget the blood and death, the screaming of horses and men alike, and the merciless slaughter when a lust of blood seems to seize your very soul and drive you to things your mind afterward pushes into its farthest recesses."

Averil stared at him, her face pale. "That does not sound like you, Lawrence."

"Does it not? Perhaps you do not really know me then, Averil." His eyes were almost veiled.

She glanced at Madoc and then down at her untouched plate of veal.

He snapped his fingers for his glass to be refilled. "You look at me, Averil, and you see an English lord in his country mansion, surrounded by all the bits and pieces that proclaim his station in life. And that is *all* you see. Isn't it?"

The moments passed and the dining room was horribly quiet.

Madoc rescued the conversation. "They tell me that O'Callaghan was a first-class man, Kendal—was that your opinion of him too?"

"Yes. He is the only reason I joined the Thirty-Ninth Regiment."

"Hardly the top-bracket regiment one associates with the nobility."

"But one of the best, for all that."

"Where are they now?"

"Canada."

"More snow and mountains, eh?" Madoc smiled.

"Their lot in life." Lawrence nodded. "But what of your lot in life, Vaughan? You do not mention army service."

"Because I have never so served, probably."

"A carpet knight?"

Madoc took a long breath. "Was that meant as offensively as it sounded?"

Lawrence looked at Corralie and then shook his head. "I meant no offense, Vaughan——it was merely a phrase. What did occupy your time during the war?"

"The Foreign Office."

"Ah—a chair-borne knight." Lawrence laughed, brushing the moment aside.

"In a manner of speaking."

"You have left the Foreign Office now?"

"Yes. And that is not in a manner of speaking; it is quite definite."

"Friction?" Lawrence leaned back, looking at him with interest.

"Most decidedly."

"Your assertion that Bonaparte would not be satisfied with Elba alone?"

Madoc smiled coolly. "Yes."

"Guaranteed to make your presence undesirable in many quarters, I fancy."

"I will be proved correct in the end—which will make my very name an anathema." Madoc looked at Corralie. "Would you think a man like Bonaparte would settle for a miniature island in the Mediterranean, Corralie?"

"If he is finished, perhaps."

"Only death will finish *l'Empereur*."

Lawrence shook his head. "They say he is become dull-witted now—playing children's games and being more and more foolish with each passing day."

"*They* perhaps would be fooled by anything."

"You're determined about him, aren't you, Vaughan?"

"I know him."

"You *know* Bonaparte?"

"In a manner of speaking." Madoc looked at Corralie. "I declare that I cannot eat another mouthful for fear of bursting—shall you eat some more or shall we walk a while on Henarth's magnificent terrace?"

Lawrence put down his glass. "We will *all* walk on the terrace."

"By all means," said Madoc, folding his napkin, "for the evening is fine and too delightful to remain indoors, don't you think, Miss Tindling?"

"Yes, Sir Madoc."

Averil had not said a word since Lawrence's unkind attack, and her face was very pale as she folded her napkin. Lawrence came around the table and pulled Corralie's chair out for her, offering her his arm. "You have not seen the new obelisk yet, have you? Had it shipped from Alexandria a few months ago. It got a bit damaged during the passage, but mostly it's just as it was when it was dug from the desert at Karnak."

"If you plunder Egypt much more, you will have all those dead pharaohs coming back to curse you, Lawrence Kendal," she said with a laugh, walking out with him. She listened to his description of the obelisk, but all the while she was wondering how to speak with Madoc.

As they crossed the terrace and descended the stone steps to the formal gardens, she linked her arm more tightly in his. "Lawrence, you can stop twittering about that cursed obelisk. We are far from my fellow guests and so you can tell me what is wrong with you tonight."

"Wrong?"

"Between you and Averil."

"Nothing."

"Then why are you so surly a beast?"

"I'm not!" he protested.

"Look me in the eye and say that."

He smiled and put a playful finger to her nose. "Keep your snout out, Corry."

"Only if you promise to behave yourself, for at the moment I am ashamed to know you." They stood by the obelisk with its incomprehensible hieroglyphics. "Anyway, Lawrence, you should be walking with Averil, not me."

"And leave Madoc Vaughan free to walk with you?"

"Why not?"

"This will lead to another argument, will it not?" he said with a smile.

"Yes."

"Then I surrender."

"*Is* something wrong, Lawrence?"

"Yes." He turned away as Madoc and Averil reached the obelisk. "And what do you think of my new acquisition, Averil?"

She looked up at it. "I don't know. What are those strange markings?"

"Ah—now that is a question I cannot answer, so that is a black mark to you for flummoxing me." He spoke gently, slipping his arm around her shoulder.

She smiled quickly at him. He looked down into her face, and Corralie saw the strange, almost hurt, expression in his eyes.

Madoc took her arm, drawing her aside. "Shall we walk a while?" he asked.

17

Madoc and Corralie walked away from the obelisk. He pulled her arm through his. "What's the matter with him tonight?"

"I think they have had an argument."

"He nearly found himself another one tonight—on the end of his well-bred nose. I've met Averil Tindling twice now, Corralie, and for the life of me I can't think why he chose her."

"Twice?"

"Once in Chacehampton with Kendal, and once in the rain with you. After tonight, I think they deserve each other."

"It's not like him, you know."

"I'll take your word for that—he's just damned English and can't help it."

"Is that the superior Welshman talking?"

"Of course. We are the master race really, only it's taking the English an unconscionable length of time to realize the fact. Now then, you wanted to talk with me?"

She looked back at the obelisk and then at the nearby maze with its shadowy entrance just visible in the light of the Chinese lanterns in the monkey puzzle trees. "We shall not be heard in there."

"Aye—but shall we ever be seen again?"

She smiled. "I hope so."

The night breeze whispered through the thick yew hedges and she could smell the distinctive perfume of the dense, dark green foliage.

He turned her to face him. "Well?"

"I don't know how to begin."

He took her hands. "Surely it cannot be so bad?"

"It is, Madoc. I have found out what uniform your brother-in-law wears in his portrait. And I was down on the beach the night the Frenchman came in—I was spying on you. So you see, it is bad, is it not?"

"Oh, sweet God, on top of everything else, this is *all* I need! Who have you told?"

"No one. Only you."

"Why have you decided to tell me what you know? What's happened?"

"I'm frightened because of the *Janus*."

"You know why she's here?"

"No. Only that they are watching for something. It could be the *Laura*, or it could be your French lugger. Either fits the bill."

He looked at her. "You heard what was said on the beach, then?"

"Yes."

"And knowing that Charles is French and that what I am up to is perhaps worthy of the navy's attention, you still tell me and no one else?"

She looked quickly away. "Yes."

"Why?" he asked gently. "Why, Corry?"

"I don't really know."

"Be honest with me."

Her eyes met his then. "All right. Because I am afraid for you, for *you*, Madoc. Because I don't want anything to happen to you."

He smiled, drawing her close. His lips were soft as he kissed her and she was almost crying as she clung to him. "You *can* trust me in all this, Corry," he whispered.

"I know."

"You trust my word so readily?"

"Yes, because I want to."

His eyes were warm as he looked at her. "What better reason, eh? Oh, Corry, I do love you so, fortune or no fortune."

"You wouldn't lie to me, would you? For I could not bear it if——"

He held her close. "I am not lying. It began in a purely mercenary way, I do not deny it, but I could not know you without loving you."

"That is not the master speaking?"

"No, it is the burbling of a man in love." He kissed her again and then released her. "And now you want to know about Charles, do you not?"

"Yes."

"He was, as you have apparently discovered, an aide-de-camp. To Marshal Grouchy, not that that has any bearing on the tale. Catti ran away to marry him secretly when Bonaparte was at the height of his power, which fact Aunt Agnes still finds intolerable. She will not mention Charles by name and has forbidden Catti to disgrace the family by broadcasting the truth of the alliance she made. When Bonaparte was defeated, Charles insisted that Catti come back to England and he insisted that she toe the family line. Catti was heartbroken at being sent back here, but Charles had a plan that could not include his British wife. When the Emperor crashed, Charles, like so many of the Imperial officers, became a Bourbon supporter—on the face of it, anyway. He exchanged his tricolor for the white cockade." Madoc smiled and raised his eyebrows. "I make this sound very melodramatic."

"Go on. Please."

"Charles also contacted me at the Foreign Office. Bonaparte had had a liking for him, and Charles knew that he would be accepted on Elba when the Emperor was relegated to that tiny backwater. It seemed then, as now, impossible that such a man as the little Corsican would ever choose to remain twiddling his restless thumbs in such a place—he *had* to rise again some day. Charles offered to desert Bourbon France and go to join Bonaparte again, even though he believed the best thing for France was the elimination of the Emperor. Oh, don't mistake me, he hasn't gone there to stick a knife in the Imperial breast. No, he has gone there to be a snake in the grass. His going to Elba makes him wanted by the royalist cause in France and therefore also by the British, being the Bourbon allies. But if the truth of his mission is discovered by Bonaparte, then his life would hang by less than the legendary thread. He is a brave man, willing to follow through to the end those things he truly believes in. I merely do all I can to aid him."

"He has gone to find out what Bonaparte's plans are?"

"Yes."

"And he has been successful?"

"I believe so. The arrangement was that when he knew anything, he would send word through Darnier's chain of cutthroats, which seems to stretch halfway around the Mediterranean and across the Channel to England. Word was sent to me here and Darnier was to wait off Elba two weeks before full moon of this month, June. But then another message came out and Charles needed to be taken off the island a month earlier. But when Darnier went there, Charles did not come."

Corralie stared. "So you don't know if he's alive or not?"

"No." He looked away. "And Catti endures the most dreadful uncertainty."

She slipped her arms around his waist and rested her head on his shoulder. "Oh, poor Catti——"

He held her. "But why the *Janus* is here, I don't know. Darnier is not likely to tell tales to his own enemies, is he? But it could be that one of his own men has a grudge. It could be anything; even that at this very moment Whitehall and the Admiralty believe the inmates of Webley Castle to be a nest of Bonapartist sympathizers. The Lord save us!" He laughed.

"Don't joke about such things."

"I wasn't."

She swallowed. "I think Chadwick's orders are about the *Laura*. I don't know why, but it's a very strong feeling I have."

"I pray you are right. But even if you are, then Chadwick's watch up on the hill could spot the *Belle Marie*. With her one red sail, she is very distinctive, and Darnier is as wanted as the *Laura*. I primed Chadwick's watch with a suitably strong cask of liquor last time, but that is hardly likely to work again."

She looked up at him. "And you did not sort Lawrence's cutter out sufficiently well, did you?" she asked quietly.

"Don't misjudge me, Corry. I don't deny that I was responsible for what happened, but only at second hand. I paid someone to have her rigging seriously meddled with, but not to cut her loose and have her almost founder on those rocks. A rogue I am, but not completely unscrupulous. Grant me that, at least. But you are right in that Lord Neptune is bound to be free to sail the seven seas, and my aunt's bay in particular, again. To think I chose Webley because it was well situated and quiet, and miraculously owned by my good self. Since Catti and I came here, the place has been running with smugglers, the navy, and lordly sea dogs!"

"And nosey women."

"Ah—but the last I welcome."

She laughed. "Well, Lawrence is unlikely to bother you on Five Warriors' Night."

"Another celebrant?"

"But of course."

"What of Harry Tindling?"

"Full-moon nights are his nights, Madoc."

"I could always scuttle him—I'm beginning to be an old hand at nefariousness. Except that I don't know where he keeps the *Laura* hidden."

"I could have helped you there——"

"You know?"

"He kept her on my father's property, on the river in Bottom Woods."

"And now?"

"She's been moved somewhere else. Father felt that Captain Chadwick had remembered that river and how deep an anchorage it was. He told Harry, and the *Laura* stole out in last night's mist."

"Damn. Do you know where?"

"No. And I could not find out for you. Harry tells no one things like that, except his crew. And sometimes Averil. But I'm sure she didn't know where the *Laura* was before."

How right you are—— Madoc gazed over her head as he held her. He would have to see Averil again, for there was a chance she might know the new hiding place. "Corry, there is something I should—confess to you."

"Yes?"

He looked down at the softness in her eyes, and he couldn't tell her. How could he expect her to accept his association with Averil Tindling? "It doesn't matter. Let's go and join our charming host."

18

It was two in the morning when the landau returned to Somerford Place. The night was clear as Corralie climbed down, and the thought of sleep was a million miles away.

She shook her head as the butler came down the steps to her. "I think I shall walk for a while, Haines. Just leave the door for me."

"Yes, Miss Corralie."

She walked slowly toward the lakes, where the fountains still played. An owl hooted somewhere in Bottom Wood and down in Chacehampton a dog was barking. Her silk skirts trailed on the grass and she could feel each tiny stone through her velvet slippers. She hugged her shawl around her shoulders, thinking of Madoc. She was in love with him and had not even realized it until tonight. Just as she had fallen out of love with Lawrence without really knowing.

She walked around the edge of the first lake, listening to the fountains and the gentle lapping of the wavelets against the ferns. As she reached the little stream that fed the lake, a new scent filled the air. The small crease the stream had made in the land was thick with creamy meadowsweet, and each breath of the night breeze released still more of the heavy, almond perfume. She walked along the bank of the stream, her skirts dragging through the tall flowers. What had Madoc called them? *Spirea ulmaria?* Meadowsweet *was* better. She gathered a bunch and hid her face in it. A real smell of summer, fresh and clean. No wonder it had been so beloved of Queen Elizabeth.

Carrying the flowers in her arms, she walked slowly back toward the house. Perhaps she would sleep now, after all.

Ellen looked disapprovingly at the meadowsweet. "Put those things in your room? Oh, Miss Corralie, they're just weeds!"

"If they were good enough for Good Queen Bess, I'm sure they're good enough for me." Corralie pushed the flowers firmly into the maid's hands. "A vase, if you please."

Ellen did as she was told, and set the vase upon the table next to the bed.

Corralie smiled. "See how fine they look against the blue brocade. A weed, indeed—they're beautiful."

"My mother took it for her indigestion."

"You are determined to ruin my enjoyment of it, aren't you. Well, my father would say it is a herb of Jupiter and therefore soothing, benevolent, and cheering."

"It will drop all over the carpet and table and make an awful mess."

"Oh, help me undress. I shall ignore your grumbling."

Ellen untied the silver string and the silk gown fell to the floor. "Did you have a good dinner, Miss Corralie?"

"It feels as if I ate half a horse—all by myself.

Lawrence will insist upon such rich foods, I wonder that he is not as fat as Prinny."

"And has he realized he's going to marry the wrong one yet?"

"Ellen!"

"Begging your pardon, Miss Corralie."

"I think they'd had a tiff anyway, if you must know."

"Good."

"Do you know, Ellen, I don't really care if they quarrel, if they marry, if they have seventeen children with bright blue hair. It doesn't matter anymore."

The maid held out a warmed nightdress, her eyes round. "Miss Corralie?"

"I'm over him."

"Then it must be because of that Welsh Sir Madoc. Oh, Miss Corralie, he's *wickedly* handsome." The maid's eyes shone appreciatively. "I saw him driving Averil in his curricle last week——"

Corralie turned slowly to look at her. "Are you sure?"

"Oh yes, Miss Corralie, they went right past me when I was coming over the stile from my sister's cottage. She was laughing at something he said, and then she said to hurry or she'd be late meeting Lord Kendal."

Corralie washed her hands and face in the bowl of warm rose water and said nothing as she climbed into the bed; but a sliver of her new happiness had flown into the night. He had lied when he had said he had only met Averil twice before tonight.

Ellen extinguished the lamp and left her. She lay there for a long while, staring at the brocade curtains, so gray and dull in the darkness. Why had he lied? She was not mistaken, for he had been so definite about it—— Her eyes were heavy, and as they closed, the last thing she saw was the vase of meadowsweet.

"Bracken!"

The trees were spinning around her again and she could hear the thunder of her own heart above the pounding of Bracken's hooves. "No!" she screamed as the stream lurched into view, and the two figures together on the bank were pale and startled. Averil's eyes were so wide and horrified, and Madoc—— As the bough swept her to the ground and the bank leaped up to meet her, she screamed again.

The night was quiet, turning gray now as the summer dawn lightened the eastern horizon. Corralie lay there, her heart still rushing from the terror of the nightmare. But it had been no nightmare. She slipped from the bed and went to the window. Her father's deer wandered slowly through the dewy grass, red shadows in the silver.

She lowered her eyes. Averil and Madoc. She had seen them that day in the woods.

And the room, like the woods, was filled with the scent of meadowsweet.

Ellen put the coffee tray on the table and shook her shoulder.

"Miss Corralie? Miss Corralie, it's past eleven o'clock. Lord Kendal has called to see you. He says it's urgent that he speak with you. Miss Corralie?"

"I'm awake, Ellen." The desolation of those early hours at dawn had not left her. She felt wretched as she got from the bed and slipped her arms into the apricot dimity robe the maid held out for her. "Is Lord Kendal with my father?"

"No, Miss Corralie. Mr. Somerford went up to his observatory a long time ago. He was meeting Lady Agnes there."

"I'll just wash my face then and have my hair brushed. Then I will go down——"

"In your wrap?"

"Yes! Oh, *Ellen*, this and my nightdress cover far more of me than my morning gowns. Don't be silly."

The maid brushed her hair so that it fell around her shoulders. "Should I tie it in a ribbon?"

"No, I have a headache. Just leave it as it is."

"Shall I bring the tray down again, then?"

"Yes, please. Where is he?"

"In the library, Miss Corralie."

"Urgent, you said?"

"Yes. He—he looks upset about something. So Haines said, anyway."

Lawrence stood by the shelves of books, his fair hair bright against the dark leather spines in their neat rows. He wore a dove-gray coat and cream-colored breeches, and the bunch of seals hanging from his waistcoat jingled as he turned to greet her.

"Corry?"

She crossed the room to him, stopping as she saw how haggard his face was. "Whatever is it, Lawrence?"

"I have no right to burden you with my problems, but I couldn't think of whom else to talk to. Forgive me."

She took his hand. "If after all these years you cannot talk to me, I would be a poor friend." *Oh, not this morning, not now when I have too many miseries of my own——*

"I will come directly to the point, then. Averil is putting horns on me."

She looked away, biting her lip, and he made her look at him again.

"You knew, didn't you?" he asked.

"I—knew servants' gossip."

"Which, as usual, is true. They're like ferrets down rabbit holes. Unerring."

"Yes." She felt as if her heart was breaking, but she held back the tears with a determination born of pride. "How long have you known?"

"A while. But I don't know who he is. Do you?"

She stared. "You don't know?"

"No. Did your servants' gossip elicit his name?"

"No."

He took his cane and walked toward the fireplace where a fresh bowl of sweet williams guarded the empty grate. "He's like some damned shadow. Twice I've seen him now, and even last night I couldn't identify him."

"Last night?" *Oh, please, no, not after all that he said to me——*

"She didn't go home after leaving Henarth." He smiled sheepishly, and sat heavily on a sofa, rubbing his leg. "I followed her. She drove in her dogcart to Bascombe Woods. I think they sensed someone was around, though, for he was leaving as I saw them at last. I didn't make my presence known, though, and he rode off and she went home in the dogcart."

"And you said nothing? Did nothing?"

"No."

"So Averil still wears your ring and doesn't know you've found her out?"

"That's right."

"But why, Lawrence? Why didn't you create a terrible scene the *first* time, let alone the second?"

"I don't know." He leaned his head back wearily. "I just don't know."

She spread her hands helplessly. "There's only one reason, isn't there? Only one possible reason. And that is that you still want her."

He smiled then and held out his hand to her, drawing her onto the sofa beside him. "Oh, Corry,

I really don't understand myself in all this. I should have rushed in that first time and made the very grandfather of all solomongrundies. But I didn't. I wanted to put her down last night in front of you and Madoc, and I tried to, but in the end I couldn't. I have behaved so vapidly as to stagger myself. I have even indulged in a notion of jealousy over your friendship with Vaughan."

She leaned her head wearily against his shoulder and closed her eyes. "A notion is all it is, too. You are only trying to make Averil jealous, aren't you? Trying to give her the impression that you might yet turn to me? You still love her, and that's why you haven't ended the engagement."

He smiled. "And so I am destined to wear countless horns?"

"I don't know. I can't help you to answer that."

"You sound more hollow than I do, Corry. I shouldn't have come making you miserable with my problems."

"I'm a little tired, that's all. What shall you do? Will you face Averil with what you know?"

He was silent for a long while and then he shook his head. "No. I'm too damned weak and foolish, and too much in love with her. I have no pride left, I fear—a humiliating discovery."

"Well, I suppose that is how I loved you for all those years, isn't it? I waited and hoped and hung on to your every word. But I lost you in the end."

"Shall I lose her, though? Or have I done so already?"

"No. If this lover of hers was going to marry her, she would have ended the engagement herself, wouldn't she?" *Madoc never intended marrying her, all he wanted was my wealth——*

"Well, having ruined your morning for you, I shall take myself into Chacehampton. Tindling's looking the *Fair Maid* over today, and I want to see exactly what's what."

She looked at him as he stood. "And if you see Averil?" she asked.

"I shall smile sweetly and greet her as always I do."

"Lawrence, you would do better to snub her, make her suffer, make her fear to lose you. I could positively *shake* you at this moment! Make her work for you, make her beaver away at winning you back. Lawrence, you're worth too much to hand yourself over on a meek little plate!"

He stared down at her. "That's *really* what you think, isn't it?"

"Yes. And if you let her do this to you without putting up a struggle, I shall despise you."

"Corry!"

"I shall—there's no getting away from that fact. No one should make themselves such easy game." *Oh, how true that is, for have I not done just that thing myself?*

"Perhaps I had better go before you stand up and bite me," he said with a little smile.

"Just go and bite Averil; show her you've got teeth."

He nodded, but she could not tell if he agreed with her or if he was just humoring her. She went with him down the wide staircase, and as Haines threw open the doors of the house, she saw that outside the summer mist was still over the countryside. It drifted clammily over the parkland, making the trees spectral and the pools and lakes impossible to see, although the musical playing of the fountains could still be heard.

She watched the cabriolet move away into the mist, and then stood there alone on the steps. What a fool she had made of herself last night with Madoc Vaughan, what an absolute and pathetic fool, clinging to his every word so eagerly. The secret of his brother-in-law was still safe with her, but she would never succumb to Madoc's easy and subtle charm again.

19

The mist was still heavy as the landau moved slowly along the lane behind Lady Agnes's barouche. Corralie sat back on the velvet seat. The last thing she felt like today was going in to Chacehampton to the new dressmaker, but there were times when Lady Agnes could insist in such a way as to make obedience by far the easier choice. "*My dear, she's a wonder, an absolute wonder. And itching, absolutely itching, to dress you. I promised I would tell you to go there. A Taurean, you know—an absolute natural at dress designing.*"

Corralie sighed. Ellen's industry with the Chinese papers and rouge had not really come off, but then there was little that face painting could achieve if the person owning the face felt so lackluster and low. And what perverse notion had it been that had insisted she wear this military pelisse of dark purple velvet which had never done anything for her? Or the military hat with its perky white cockade? If ever anyone had set out today determined to look her worst, it was Miss Corralie Somerford.

She was roused from her thoughts by the change of sound as the landau turned onto the quayside and rattled over the cobbles. Torches had been lit on the ships moored in the harbor, and the smoke from them only added to the mist. As Corralie stepped down she noticed the unnatural quiet. There was no wind and the sea lapped eerily against the harbor walls, and the seagulls were silent too. She could see several of them perched upon the masts of a schooner, and they made little sounds to one another, but there was none of their usual screeching and wailing. The fishing boats rocked at their moorings, their crews standing idly, waiting for the mist to lift.

Lady Agnes opened the door of the barouche and looked out. "Well, in you go then, Corralie, and be sure you take your time and choose carefully. Are you *sure* you're feeling well?"

"Yes, Lady Agnes, thank you. Now you go on back home and don't worry about me any more."

"If you're sure——"

"Yes, perfectly sure." *Oh, please go and leave me alone——*

The door closed and the barouche moved off, vanishing into the swirling mist. The lantern by the dressmaker's window crackled a little and Corralie turned to get back into the landau and return home.

It was then that she saw Averil. She was standing at the doorway of the shoemaker's examining a pair of kid shoes. The shoemaker stood anxiously beside her, his spectacles perched on the end of his long nose and his leather apron almost touching the ground. How elegant Averil looked, so dainty in her high-waisted muslin gown and tight blue spencer. Corralie watched the girl until she and the shoemaker turned to go back into the shop. Averil and Madoc. Her heart twisted.

The Beau snorted close by and she looked up at the rider. "Madoc!"

He smiled. "I was coming to call upon you when I almost rode into your landau."

"Oh."

"Are you coming in or going out?"

Her heart almost twisted as she looked up at him, but she would *not* give in to her love. "I was going into Miss Yelverton's. I shall be some time so——"

"So, I will come in with you." He dismounted and looped The Beau's reins over a post.

"No."

He looked at her. "Don't you want my company, then?"

"No."

"What's wrong, Corry?"

"Nothing. If you will excuse me——"

"No, I will not. I will not be snubbed, Corry, not by you."

She went to the door of the shop and pushed it open. The bell tinkled and the proprietress hurried forward. "Oh, it's Miss Somerford, isn't it? Lady Agnes said that she would tell you of my humble establishment."

"Yes. Yes, she told me. May I see your design books, please?" Corralie was shaking as she went to sit in the little pink satin chair by the counter. She did not look up from her lap as the bell went again.

Madoc leaned against the counter, removing his top hat and putting it next to him. Slowly he loosened his gloves and then tossed them into the hat. He said nothing as the dressmaker and her assistant brought the design books, and then he smiled sweetly at Miss Yelverton.

"If you will leave us, please."

"Oh. Oh, yes, of course, sir." The woman patted her mobcap nervously, glancing at Corralie's pale face and then at Madoc again. "If you need me, just touch that bell on the counter there."

"But of course." He bowed his head politely, smiling at her in a way that disarmed her completely.

In some confusion, the woman ushered her assistant away and the door into the back of the shop closed softly behind them.

"Now, Corry. What is all this nonsense about? Mm?"

She turned the pages of the first book and looked without seeing anything. "I have nothing to say to you."

He lifted his foot suddenly and pushed the design book's cover over so that it closed with a snap. "Oh, yes you have. I'm no damned servant, Corry. You will do me the honor of telling me what is wrong."

"*Honor*—I wonder you can spit out such a word." The shaking was worse now, and she opened the book again.

He stared at her. "Being shut out so completely and not to be told the reason why is a little unfair, is it not?"

"You know what is wrong, Madoc, you damned well know!" She looked at him then. "Unless, of course, your faults and deceptions are so legion that you are really at a loss to decide which ones I may have chanced upon!"

There was a ghost of a smile on his lips. "You have remembered, haven't you?"

"Yes."

"I was hoping that that blank would remain blissfully blank."

"No doubt."

"Because I love you, Corry."

She shook her head slowly. "Oh, no—don't try that tack again, Madoc. Not ever again. You don't love me, you want my wealth to feather your nest with. And as Averil cuckolds Lawrence, so you would cuckold me."

"That isn't how it is."

"Isn't it?" She stood. "So, it's all over, is it? You won't see her again?"

"It never was, damn it—not like that. I tried to tell you last night, but couldn't."

She looked scornfully at him. "And after seeing me, you went to meet her again. Don't try to fool me anymore, for I will not be fooled. You may kiss farewell to any hopes you may have had of me, because there is nothing left in me for you. I despise you, and loathe you for the worm that you are. Goodbye, Madoc."

Outside, the mist had thickened so that she could not even see the landau. She hesitated for a moment, blinded both by the mist and by the tears which had had their way at last.

He caught her arm as she took the first step from the doorway and dragged her to the side of the building where some huge bales of hay had been stacked.

"Corry, I won't let it rest at that!"

"Take your hands off me. You cannot deny that you kissed me last night and then went to meet Averil, can you? Can you?"

"No."

"Then there is nothing more to be said, is there?"

"Yes. I told you no lies last night, Corry——"

"You did—you said that you had only met Averil twice before. You omitted to mention the joy ride you and she took in your curricle. My maid saw you."

"And who saw us last night, then?"

She gave a short laugh. "Lawrence did."

He released her. "I didn't want that to happen."

"No, you just wanted to enjoy Averil and enjoy

my wealth at the same time. How sad that your plans have gone awry."

"Don't use that tone with me, Corry."

"I know of no other way to speak to you now."

"I had to see her for one last time, Corry. I needed to find out where her father had taken his cutter."

"Oh, come *on*, Madoc. You will have to do better than that! How feeble an explanation to try foisting upon me. Oh, you're the great swell, aren't you? Coming here and almost convincing me of your honesty and worth. I must have been crack-brained to let you make such a fool of me."

He looked helplessly at her. "I didn't make a fool of you—I *love* you! I tried to tell you about Averil, I was on the point of it, but I couldn't. I knew you wouldn't believe me, I suppose."

"And how right you were!" She went to move past him, but he caught her and pulled her back.

"Corry, please——"

"Your secrets are safe with me, Madoc. I will tell no one of what you said last night concerning Charles Beauchamp, but as to the rest, I want nothing more to do with you. I do not want you to speak to me, to call upon me, or ever to contact me again. Now, release me, for I wish to go."

He held her roughly, pulling her into his arms and kissing her. His lips were so warm and loving that she could so nearly have relented and put her arms around him, as in her heart of hearts she still wanted to do——

He dropped his arms and looked at her. "So, there is nothing left, is there? Your words may say that, but you are not consummate enough an actress to prove it through and through, are you?"

She looked past him at the bales of hay. "You may believe what you wish, Madoc."

He stared at her for a long moment and then nodded. "Very well. Goodbye, Corralie."

She did not answer, and he left her there on the misty quay.

20

Reynold and Corralie walked slowly into the late afternoon sun. The deer hardly stirred from their grazing as the two passed through the herd, and Reynold looked proudly at them.

"Fine beasts, eh, Corry? Look at that young buck over there. See him? I'll warrant he's as fine a specimen as any you'll find." He glanced at his quiet daughter. "Are you listening?"

"I beg your pardon?"

"Whatever's the matter with you? I can't get a word out of you these days—it's like squeezing water from a stone."

"I'm sorry. What were you saying?"

"Oh, God, it doesn't matter. Did you notice old Chadders' men creeping around Bottom Wood the other day? Eh? I knew I was right, you know—that old stoat had remembered fishing down there all those years ago. Well, we were too sharp for him, eh? Do you know, I couldn't resist it—I took meself to Chacehampton this morning and got 'Zekiel to row me out to the *Janus*. Asked Chadders point blank why he'd been snooping around."

She stopped. "You didn't!"

"Why not? He hadn't found anything, had he? I just couldn't resist the temptation. Oh, a sweet moment."

"What did he say?"

"Oh, that that was why the *Janus* is here, to look for the *Laura* and sink her, and to catch Tindling and his men red-handed if possible. It was that business with the Revenue cutter, don't you know? Too many red faces after that escapade—Harry's name is synonymous with the Revenue's failure. They had to ask the navy for help. That's why he's here, watching and waiting."

They walked on. She picked a low-hanging rhododendron as they passed a vast bush. The flowers were so crisp and beautiful. She stared at the mauve-pink petals thoughtfully. She had stumbled upon a piece of information Madoc would dearly like to possess——

Reynold chuckled to himself. "Poor old Chadders, his face was a picture. Haven't seen him like that since the day he got caught climbing the church tower to retrieve his breeches from the flagpole. Damme, that was a time. Going back a bit, mind. Still, I told Harry what I'd found out——"

"You false friend."

"Well, I don't want to lose me supply of cognac, do I? Anyway, Chadders won't catch the *Laura*."

"Don't be so sure. The *Janus* is very fast and the *Laura* is getting on."

"She'll still show a clean pair of heels to the navy, don't you fret. I didn't tell you, did I? Harry brought her back to the Bottom Wood anchorage yesterday in that early mist. Chadders is done with snooping around her, so she'll be as snug as a bug in the proverbial."

"The *Laura* is back here?"

"Yes, what safer place is there now?"

"None, I suppose."

"Corry, you're damned odd these days. Are you sure you're not ailing? Perhaps Yattere should take a look at you again."

"I'm perfectly all right!"

"Don't snap me head off—you're as jumpy as Harry's men. They took a shot at *me* this morning when I went down there unexpectedly. The *Janus*'s presence has made them like nuts in a fire."

She stared at him. "They nearly shot you?"

"Yes—I was fool enough to go down there by the long path in the half-light. They thought I was a spy or something. Shoot first, ask questions afterward." He grinned. "Shaved past me new periwig though, a bit too close for any man's comfort." He took a long, satisfying breath of the evening air. "By all the gods, this is a fine evening. If I were a younger man, I'd be out riding now. A good horse and nothing to do but ride. Corry, you should get out on that new mare of yours—she'll be too fresh if you leave her."

"I know."

"Take her out for an hour now, put some roses back in your blasted white cheeks."

"I don't really feel like riding."

"Good God, girl. Vaughan didn't give you that beast so that you could leave her in her stall all the time. Go on, now. Get yourself togged for riding and put your miseries behind you for a while. I refer to the miseries you're deliberately not telling your old father about."

She smiled and kissed him. "They're nothing you can help me with, anyway. I'll do as I'm told now and take Pippit out."

She rode easily along the lane toward Chacehampton; perhaps her father had been right after all, and a ride would do her good. She urged the mare along the wide grass verge toward the corner where a huge old oak hung over the lane as it twisted down toward the crossroads. The barouche seemed to be there all of a sudden, its broken wheel making it lean at a precarious angle. Corralie reined Pippit in and stared at Catti, who was standing by the coachman inspecting the wheel.

"Catti! Are you all right?"

"Yes, Corralie. But I fear Aunt Agnes's barouche is not."

"Is it just the wheel?"

"We think so." Catti held Pippit's bridle and looked up at Corralie. "I know it's none of my concern——"

"That's right, it isn't. Forgive me if I'm rude, Catti, but I really don't want to talk about it."

"But Corralie——" Catti led the mare away from the coachman, who could hear every word. "Corralie, Madoc loves you."

"No. He loves my prospects."

"That isn't so." Tears hung in Catti's eyes. "Oh, this is all my fault, and I cannot forgive myself."

"Your fault?"

"It was my idea in the first place."

"I don't understand."

"I don't mean that the whole thing was my idea, just—just that Madoc should try to find things out through Averil. Oh dear, it sounds so very reprehensible doesn't it? But you see, Corralie, we knew that there was bad feeling between Averil's father and Darnier, and so it was imperative really to try to keep the *Laura* from sailing when the *Belle Marie* was due. So Madoc took to going in to Chacehampton in the evenings, to the taverns, the market place, the quay, and so on, just to try to overhear something that might tell us where the *Laura* was. But that was so dangerous really, for if they realized what he was trying to find out—well, I don't like to think about what could have happened to my brother. I love him very much indeed, Corralie, for he is the most gentle and kind brother ever a woman had." Catti smiled and released the bridle. "You must believe that."

"I have no reason not to."

"I am trying to put things right for him. With you. Corralie, we were in Chacehampton one morning and we met Lord Kendal and Averil, and I could see that Averil was very taken with Madoc. It seemed obvious to me then what we should do, and I put it to Madoc that he should—well, that he should court Averil, and so that is what he did. He doesn't love her, Corralie. He never has and he never will. He has done this for Charles's sake and for no other reason. He told me that he was afraid you might discover the truth. He *does* love you."

And I love him—but I cannot trust him——

Catti stared up at the silent girl. "You are making this hard for me."

"What can I say? He lied to me. He told me he loved me and then went straight away to meet Averil. I cannot accept that, Catti. I'm sorry."

"It was the last time, for she did not know where the *Laura* was, anyway. And in a few days the *Belle Marie* will come—pray God Charles will be aboard." Catti searched in her reticule for her handkerchief, blinking back the tears.

Corralie reached down to put her hand on the girl's shoulder. "Forgive my surly manner, Catti, please. I feel I have been made to look foolish by your brother, and I cannot help how I feel. But anyway, I have some news to ease your mind. The *Janus* is here simply and solely to watch for the *Laura*, my father found out from Captain Chadwick. And—and the *Laura* is back at her berth in Bottom Wood. I only learned a short while ago."

Catti closed her eyes with relief. "Oh, thank God, thank God——" But then her eyes flew open and she looked up quickly. "But Madoc is going in to Chacehampton tonight, to follow Harry Tindling. Averil told him that her father was going to the *Laura* tonight." She stared helplessly at the wheel of the barouche. "And I cannot stop him. Corralie, I did not want him to go tonight, because I know it is too dangerous."

"When is he leaving Webley?"

"Half past ten. When it is dark."

Corralie looked at her fob watch. It was half past nine. "I suppose I could reach Webley before he leaves——"

"Would you, Corralie? Oh please, I don't want him to risk his life by doing what he plans. I begged him to stay safely at Webley." The tears shone in Catti's eyes. "If you won't help Madoc, then please help me."

"I will ride as swiftly as I dare, Catti. I promise." Corralie kicked her heel and Pippit moved easily past the barouche and on down the lane toward the crossroads.

21

Lady Agnes put down her basket of dried herbs and beamed. "Why, Corralie, what a delightful surprise. And at such a late hour."

There was no sign of Madoc anywhere. "I—I came to tell you that Catti's barouche has broken down. I came upon her on the road above the crossroads, on the Cannutbury side. Someone will have to go and rescue her."

"Oh, good heavens—she's all right?"

"Yes."

"I'll send Drew out with the chaise immediately. Thank you for coming to tell me, Corralie."

"Is Madoc here?"

"No. He went to Chacehampton some time ago. He had an appointment with—do you know, I can't for the life of me think what he said now. I was so intent upon sorting my herbs that his words just went over my head, I fear."

Corralie's heart fell. She was too late. "Well, I must be getting back, or Father will be wondering——"

"Wait, and Drew can go with you. I would be a lot happier."

"No, thank you. I am riding Pippit, and it will be far quicker if I just take myself home. Good night, Lady Agnes." She bent to kiss the old lady's cheek.

"Good night, my dear. And take care now."

"I will."

Corralie hurried down the stone steps into the courtyard and took Pippit's reins from the groom. As she rode out beneath the old gatehouse, she could not think what to do next. She had little hope of finding Madoc in Chacehampton, for he was hardly likely to advertise his presence.

She urged Pippit down the high-banked lane. If Madoc followed Harry, then inevitably he would reach Bottom Wood. But if Harry or his men should discover him—— She kicked her heel again and Pippit leaped forward. *I must think of something——*

The deer fled as Pippit crossed the grounds of Somerford Place, and at the stable yard she dismounted. "Gerry? *Gerry!*"

"Yes, Miss Corralie."

"See to Pippit for me." She gathered her cumbersome riding habit and hurried into the house.

"Ellen?"

"Miss Corralie?"

"Get my blue muslin out. Quickly!"

"But, Miss Corralie——"

"Don't argue, just get it out. Oh damn these stupid little buttons!"

"Here, let me do it, Miss Corralie. But why do you want to dress again? It's very late now."

"Don't ask and you'll be told no fibs. Where's my father?"

"In the attics."

"*Where?*"

"The attics. He's remembered some old book he put up there years ago and has gone to look for it.

There, that's the thing undone. Here's the blue muslin."

"Oh, hurry!"

"I'm being as quick as I can, Miss Corralie," protested the maid.

Corralie stepped into the flimsy gown and tied the drawstring quickly. "Is my hair too bad?"

"A little windswept."

"Brush it, then. No, just loose, no pins and prinking. That's it. And the black ribbons. There. Now, I'm going out for a while, Ellen."

"But where, Miss?"

"Not far. Don't tell my father. Let him think I am in the bathhouse or something."

"Yes, Miss Corralie."

Corralie snatched her white shawl and hurried down the stairs, leaving the bewildered maid standing on the landing.

Bottom Wood seemed so far away as she hurried down the sloping lawns. The plan half-formed in her mind was as flimsy as the foolish gown, but was all she could think of.

The breeze moaned through the trees as she halted on the edge of the wood, drawing the shawl more tightly around her shivering shoulders. It wasn't cold, but her teeth were chattering. The house looked so comforting behind her, with its lights twinkling. She held her breath for a moment and then went on down the half-hidden path toward the river.

In a clearing where a fallen elm lay rotting among the undergrowth, she stopped. She must begin now. Crossing her fingers, she called out. "Madoc?" She called loudly, hoping that the sound would reach Harry Tindling and his men, who must surely be down by the *Laura.*

Silence greeted her. The trees rustled and the

leaves all around her trembled as the wind breathed over the wood. She called again. "Madoc? Where are you?" She walked on, pushing noisily past bushes and making no attempt at all to be secret. Through the tress ahead she saw the glint of moonlight on the river.

Suddenly a man blocked the path in front of her. Harry folded his huge arms across his chest, staring suspiciously at her.

"What you want, Miss Corralie? You've no business coming down here tonight."

"I'm looking for Sir Madoc Vaughan. I am afraid for him."

He did not smile or look in the least bit friendly. "What's he doing here, then?"

"We—we were walking together." She looked as flustered and embarrassed as she could manage. "I was meeting him secretly, Harry, and I did not realize until just now that the *Laura* was back. I had an argument with him and left him down here somewhere, and suddenly I thought that he doesn't know his way around here in the daytime let alone in the dark. I got frightened that he might accidentally come across the *Laura*. Has he, Harry? Please tell me."

"Just with you, was he?"

"Yes."

"It's as well for him that you came back, then."

"You've caught him?"

Harry nodded slowly. "But we've done nothing to him. Yet."

"He's my friend, Harry. He wasn't snooping." The smuggler said nothing, and Corralie's heart began to thunder. "Please believe me, Harry. *I* wouldn't have any reason to lie to you, would I? Let him go."

Harry studied her face for a long while and then at last he nodded. "I'll trust your word, Miss Corralie—*yours*, mind, and if anything bad comes of this, then on your head be it."

She swallowed. "Yes."

"Bide here, then, and I'll bring him to you."

As silently as he had appeared, Harry vanished down the path again. Corralie's hands twisted and twisted, tying and untying the fringe of her shawl. It seemed an endless wait as she stood there on the dark path listening to the night sounds of the woodland around her.

Harry and Madoc walked slowly toward her and as she ran toward Madoc, she prayed he would have the wit to follow her lead. "Oh, Madoc, I was so afraid for you." She flung her arms around him and held him tightly.

He did not hesitate, but held her close. "I'm all right, sweetheart."

"And all for such a foolish argument." She looked up at him.

A flicker of a smile passed through his dark eyes. "Aye, that it surely was, a very foolish argument."

Harry stood there. "Silent tongue and still, mind, or you'll meet your end at my hands yet, Sir Fancy Vaughan. You've got Miss Corralie to thank for your hide tonight."

Madoc nodded. "Oh, I shall thank her properly, have no fear."

Harry grinned unexpectedly. "I'll warrant you will, an' all. Now get on out of here, both on you."

Madoc took Corralie's hand and led her up the path past the fallen elm. They walked in silence and did not stop until they reached the edge of the wood. There, he caught her close and held her. She could feel the slight trembling of his body.

He kissed her. "Sweet God, I thought I was not long for this world tonight."

She was almost crying. "So did I—and I could not bear it."

He put his hand to her chin and tilted her face toward him. "Am I forgiven, then? Do you love me again?"

"Oh, Madoc, I did not really stop loving you."

"I tell you this, Miss Corralie Somerford, you certainly had me convinced to the contrary. I would not have come to you again."

She stretched up to kiss him tenderly. "I know," she whispered. "And I cannot bear *that* thought, either."

"But how did you know where I was?"

"I met Catti. When I knew where you'd gone, I was terrified for you, for my father was nearly shot here this morning. Harry is not a man to stop and ask politely for your business before he shoots you. I could only think of looking for you and pretending—well you know the rest." She smiled. "I even changed into this dress to make it look more convincing."

"You risked a great deal for me tonight, didn't you?"

"I love you," she said simply.

He ran his fingers through her thick, dark red hair. "And I love you, Corry. Now, let's get ourselves safely away from here." He kissed her fingertips and they walked back toward the house.

22

Reynold was coming down the stairs as Corralie and Madoc came in. He looked over the bannisters short-sightedly.

"Upon me soul, Vaughan! Corry? It's a trifle late for calling, ain't it?"

"Your pardon, Mr. Somerford. We had not realized the time." Madoc smiled.

"I see—that's the way of it, is it? Well, at least her expression is a little sweeter. Well, come on up, then. I can't abide chit-chatting from one floor to the next." He dusted the book he had under his arm and then vanished from view in the direction of the library.

They followed him and found him pouring some Madeira. "You—er, you weren't in the vicinity of Bottom Wood, I trust."

"Yes, Father."

"Corry, I *told* you what nearly happened to me, and you choose to go there at night? I despair of your intelligence sometimes."

"Well, all was well, anyway."

"Corry—what's going on, eh? You went out riding in a pale green habit, as I recall—and yet now you have apparently just wandered back in from walking with Vaughan here, and you are garbed in pale blue muslin. I know my dotage is approachin', but I don't think I'm that far gone yet. Well?"

Madoc took the glass of Madeira offered to him. "Well, it's very involved."

"The night is young, dear boy—and I can sit and listen to my heart's content." Reynold motioned Corralie into the nearest chair and then sat down himself. "I'm all ears."

Madoc ran his fingers through his hair and looked at Corralie. She smiled. "You'd better tell him. He'll only be a nuisance if you don't."

"That's hardly a way to talk of your father, my girl," said Reynold huffily.

"Well, you will. Once you get a notion in your head, you're the very devil."

He beamed beatifically. "I long ago discovered that in this particular household that was the perfect way of keeping a finger on the proverbial pulse. You tell me things in the end because I'm a pest. Now then, Vaughan."

Madoc nodded. "Very well." He sat down and told Reynold all about Charles Beauchamp and the expected arrival of the *Belle Marie* on Five Warriors' Night. He told him almost everything—he omitted to mention Averil.

"So that's why you were in Bottom Wood, eh? Snooping. Damned dangerous and fool thing to do, you know. Harry's not engaged on arranging a tea party."

"I realize that."

"And I can tell you one thing for nothing. He hasn't made up his mind about Five Warriors' Night yet. Half his crew want to join in the junketings, the other half are prepared to sail with him. But the *Laura* needs more than half a crew. That's how it stands at the moment."

"Which is hardly helpful."

"No." Reynold rubbed his chin thoughtfully. "And you can't go cutting ropes or damaging her now, either. You've been found in Bottom Wood. Anything happening to her now would point sweetly and certainly in your direction."

Madoc glanced at Corralie. "I know."

"Let me see, it's ten days to Five Warriors', ain't it? There's time enough."

"For what?" asked Corralie.

"To find out finally what he intends doing. I shall ask him, damn it. I can say Chadwick's coming to dine—anything to open up the matter. If he's not sailing, that'll be the end of it. But if he is——"

"Yes?"

"Well, you can always put to him the story you've just put to me."

Madoc stared. "And expect Harry Tindling to listen?"

"Yes. Mind—we'd have to doctor the tale somewhat. Tell him your brother-in-law's landing for some other reason. Damn it, if he thought Boney was going to be on the loose again, he'd be cock-a-hoop. Business is bad when there's peace, but with war again the price of cognac would shoot through the roof. Which makes me inquire why this Darnier is so keen to help, being in the same line of business, so to speak."

"Bonaparte has a particular quarrel with him—I don't know the nature of it, but it's sufficient to make Darnier keen to keep Bonaparte safely on Elba. Or safely shackled somewhere else. He doesn't care particularly, merely that Bonaparte does not start up again."

"That explains it. Right. Leave it with me. It will be no hardship for me to find out what Harry's up to; he trusts me."

Corralie smiled at him. "And when you speak

with him, please come the heavy father about discovering I was in Bottom Wood with Madoc, won't you? He'll believe you even more than me."

"I know—a winning old rogue, am I not?" He reached across and patted her hand. "Mind you, I'm not very pleased to find that you've been spreading gossip about yourself like that. It'll be buzzed all over Chacehampton, you know."

Madoc finished his glass. "Oh, I am more than ready to make an honest and reputable woman of her, Mister Somerford. And a real titled lady, for what that's worth." He smiled at her.

Reynold nodded. "That, my boy, is between the pair of you. I'm for my bed. All these late nights will be the end of me." He dropped a kiss on Corralie's head, nodded at Madoc, and then left the library, pausing only to pick up the precious book he'd spent so long searching for.

Madoc looked at her. "I had best get myself home, too, or Catti will be in a ferment about me. Corry, about Averil——"

"I must learn to live with it, mustn't I? If I want you." She stood and slipped her arms around his waist. "And I *do* want you."

He kissed her softly. "I will go before those baser instincts seize me again. I love you, Corry."

She held him tightly for a moment and then he left. She heard his steps descending the staircase and then the door closed. From the window she watched him cross the park toward the icehouse where he had hidden The Beau.

She was about to leave the window when something moved by the stables. It was a woman, her hood pulled over her head. The shadowy figure hovered by the clock tower and then pulled the hood back from her face. It was Averil.

On impulse, Corralie ran from the room and down the stairs to find Haines supervising the bolting of the front doors. "No, Haines! Open them again if you please!"

"Yes, Miss Corralie."

The bolts seemed to take an age, but at last the doors swung open and she ran outside.

Averil was caught unawares, turning sharply as Corralie approached.

"Did you want something, Averil?"

The girl studied Corralie's face, seeing the shining light in her eyes and the air of happiness that still pervaded her. The confusing jealousy and mixture of fascination and guilt Averil felt for Madoc bubbled up inside her, and the light in Corralie's eyes seemed suddenly to be mocking. A dull, painful color spread over Averil's face. "So it's funny is it, Corralie? It amuses you to think how humiliated I am?"

"No, don't ever think that——"

"I do, though. I think it very much. Well, you won't have the last laugh, Corralie, and Madoc Vaughan won't make me the laughing stock of Chacehampton."

"We're not laughing at you, Averil."

"Oh, so you *do* know all about my meetings with him?"

"Yes."

Averil's eyes glittered unpleasantly. "Love him, do you?"

"Yes."

"Well, I'll see to it that you don't marry him. Do you hear me?"

Corralie stared. "Look to your own future, Averil, and forget about mine. Think of keeping Lawrence Kendal, not keeping me from Madoc."

"I won't let this pass, Corralie. No one makes up to me and all the while courts someone else. No one, do you hear me? I watched him kissing you just now, up there in the library, and my father told me you and Madoc had been meeting secretly down in the woods. Well, one good turn deserves another. I shall tell your father that Madoc is no fit man to marry you, and I shall tell him exactly why."

"You'd do that? You'd risk all that just to get your own back, like any spoilt child?"

"I'd do it, yes. Lawrence Kendal is not worth keeping. I don't care about him anymore. His moods leave me not knowing how he is going to be when I see him, and then his gentleness makes me feel like screaming at other times. He's an ineffectual toad, and sometimes I think I despise him. I don't care if he ends his engagement to me."

Corralie could do nothing but stare at the girl's tormented face. Averil pulled her hood up over her hair again and spoke to the silent figure in blue muslin. "There's one thing your father cannot stand, Corralie, and that is scandal. There's a thing or two in his past that he's struggled to keep secret—my father's told me. So you may forget your hope of wedding Madoc Vaughan. I shall see to that."

With that she turned and hurried across the dark lawns, her slippers making little sounds on the grass.

23

The following morning Corralie awoke early, if indeed she had really slept all night. She slipped from the bed.

"Ellen?"

"Yes, Miss Corralie? I have not set out your clothes yet——"

"It's all right. Is my father awake? I know he rises with the sun."

"Well, he's awake, Miss Corralie. He's having his morning cup of tea in his bed."

"I'll go and see him, then. No, no, don't worry about my things. I realize I'm rather early for me. Just my wrap."

She tied the dimity wrap around her waist and took a long breath. She had thought about Averil's threat and there was no doubt that she had meant what she said. There seemed only one way to perhaps take a little of the sting from her, and that was to tell Reynold first.

"Father?"

The door stood a little open and she saw him sitting in his bed, his nightcap pulled forward over his balding head. He jumped, snapping the book closed abruptly and pushing it beneath the dull brown coverlet.

"What are you creeping about so early for, eh? Giving poor old men heart attacks in their beds."

"I don't know what you're looking so jittery for, I only greeted you." She sat on the edge of the bed.

He sniffed and cleared his throat. "Well? What've you got to say? I want to be up and over at the observatory soon."

"To meet Lady Agnes for another erudite discussion?"

"As a matter of fact, no. Not that it's your concern."

"Now who's being tetchy? If you are in a bad mood, I think I will not tell you what I came to say, for it is too delicate a matter for your ill humor."

He smiled then. "I'm sorry. What is it?"

"It's about what Madoc said last night."

"You want to accept him, don't you?"

"Yes."

"But——?"

"But. Oh, Lord, there isn't an easy way of saying this."

Reynold frowned. "He's not got you with child, has he?"

"*No!*"

"I'd wring his blasted neck with me bare hands!"

"It's nothing like that. It doesn't even directly concern me."

"Spit it out, girl."

"Madoc has been seeing Averil Tindling."

His mouth dropped. "But she's been engaged to Lawrence since before Vaughan came to Webley."

"I know."

"She's been playing Lawrence double, has she?"

Corralie looked away. "He was trying to find out where the *Laura* was."

Reynold raised a withering eyebrow. "Corry, the other foot plays 'Rule Britannia.' If he's really convinced you of that rubbish, then I take me hat off to him for the clever liar he is. Why tell me, though, eh?"

"Because Averil threatened to tell you herself."

"Oh, hell and a woman scorned, is it? Well, you're not marrying the fellow, Corry, and that's the end of it."

Corralie studied his face. "Is there no scandal in your murky past, then? Have you led so blameless a life that you can sit there and pass judgment on Madoc?"

Reynold flushed, his eyes flashing angrily. "My past has nothing to do with this! I am in a position to pass judgment on whomsoever I please, and it pleases me to condemn Vaughan! He's been the architect of his own fate in this, hasn't he? Not content with you, he had to make up to Averil as well. Whatever his reasons, they don't matter to me, madam! Well, *I* won't have it, d'you hear?"

"I hear. But I still love him."

"That don't signify. He's a coxcomb and he's not getting his mittens on *my* money. And you're not getting involved in any scandal which seems about to break over our heads. *No!* Don't look at me like that, for I'll not be moved on it. If he's been messing with Averil, then let him marry her and make good the damage he's done."

She stood. "And if *I* still want to marry him?"

"Don't push me to that, Corry. I love you dearly, but I'll not have a man like that beneath my roof."

Without another word she went to the door, but he called her. "I don't give much for his chances, anyway."

"What do you mean?"

"If she squeals like a stuck pig, Harry'll tear him to pieces. You may depend upon it. And I, for one, would stand by."

Averil stood on the quay looking down at the *Fair Maid*. She did not see Lawrence until he spoke just behind her.

"There was less damage than we thought," he said.

"Lawrence." Her voice was flat.

"Won't you come aboard and take a glass with me?" He smiled.

She concealed her irritation. "I was going to Miss Yelverton's."

"A fitting for your wedding gown? There is time enough. She won't say anything about so important a customer being late." He took her hand and led her along the gangplank and down into the luxurious cabin of the cutter. He closed the door, turning the key.

"Now then, Averil, I believe we have some things to talk about, don't we?"

Fear passed over her. There was a hardness about him she had sensed once before, at the dinner party. "Things?"

"Your lover, to be precise."

"I have no lover!" Her eyes were huge with sudden dread.

"I have the witness of my own eyes to give the lie to that, sweetheart. On two occasions I have seen you with him, and on the first occasion you spent an embarrassingly long time alone in your father's house. Embroidering, I presume?"

Her heart almost stopped within her, and she glanced at the door. He smiled, removing the key and dropping it into his waistcoat pocket.

"Lawrence—I shall scream, I shall call for my father unless you let me leave this instant."

"Scream if you wish—I have already informed Harry that you and I have some disturbing problems to chew over and that the meal may be a little noisy."

"What did you tell him?"

"That your attention has been wandering. No more than that."

"I've done nothing. Nothing."

"You've been guilty of kissing another man, again I have the witness of my own eyes to tell me that. Who is he, Averil?"

He spoke so quietly. She stared at him, her eyes large and frightened. She could not tell him that it was Madoc, for there was murder in his face as he watched her. "He's gone now, he's left Chacehampton, I promise you. I didn't do anything, I'm still——"

"A virgin?"

"Yes. I have not dishonored you, Lawrence."

"Who was he?"

She searched the cabin for inspiration and her glance fell on a book. "Keble. John Keble. He was a friend of Corralie's." Immediately she regretted the last sentence.

He raised his eyebrow. "That is easily checked, is it not?"

She nodded miserably.

"And so, this *affaire de coeur* is over?"

"Yes." She took the ring from her finger and placed it before him on the table. "I know you want this."

"No."

She looked up quickly. "But——"

"I want you, Averil. I asked you to marry me and I still want you that way—as my wife."

"After all that I've just confessed to you?"

"Yes. But you'll be faithful from now on, Averil, or you will regret the day you were born. And you will prove to me at this very moment how loving and sweet you intend being."

"Now?" she breathed, staring at him.

He nodded. "We are about to begin again, and I shall no longer be treating you as if you are made of crystal. Gentleness seems to gain little of your respect." He held out his hand. "Come to me."

He was a stranger. The soft, meek Lawrence she had come to despise had gone—— Her fingers curled around his and he gripped them. "If you ever deceive me again——"

"I won't," she whispered. "I promise that. I'll be good, Lawrence." She lifted her face toward his. Suddenly she was praying that he did not discover the truth, that it had been Madoc; she didn't want him to know. Not anymore.

Corralie was looking at Miss Yelverton's design books again. "Yes, I think this one. Have you any sprigged muslin?"

"Why, yes, of course. There is a very fine Indian muslin—in leaf green, or in pink. And white, of course, always in white."

The door bell tinkled and Corralie glanced up. Averil halted in surprise. "Corralie?"

Corralie gazed at her curiously. She had flushed cheeks—and a look in her eyes. There was a strange air about her.

"Corralie, I——" Averil looked pointedly at the unfortunate dressmaker. "Would you excuse us for a moment, Miss Yelverton?"

"Of course." The woman looked a little displeased, but still managed a polite smile before leaving the two women.

"What do you want, Averil?"

"I—I have to beg something of you."

"Beg? Of *me*? Good heavens." Corralie flicked a page of the design book.

"I know you have no cause to do anything for me, especially after last night. But—it's different now."

Corralie looked up. "Is it?"

"Yes."

"You've seen Lawrence, haven't you?"

"Yes." Averil flushed. "I won't make trouble for you. Not any more."

Corralie closed her eyes faintly. "It's too late. I've made the trouble for myself, with my clacking, interfering tongue. I told my father this morning, thinking I would forestall you."

"You told him everything?"

"Yes."

Averil's hands tightened on the handle of her parasol. "That it was with Madoc?"

"Yes."

"He'll tell Lawrence."

"I doubt it. My father is concerned only with preventing me from marrying Madoc. He couldn't care less about you and Lawrence."

"Beg him for me, Corralie—beg him not to tell Lawrence!"

"It's that important to you now, is it?"

"Yes."

"It took you long enough to see him truly, Averil Tindling."

Averil looked at her. "I doubt that even you have seen him truly, Corralie."

"Well, put it this way—I doubt very much whether I would have been so completely surprised as you seem to be. Lawrence is no milksop. I would not have loved him for long if he had been. But what was it you wanted to ask of me?"

"I have lied to him. I was frightened of what he would do and—I lied. I told him that the man I had been seeing was a friend of yours. A man named John Keble."

"And Lawrence believed you?"

"Yes."

Corralie raised her eyebrows. "I wonder."

"He did!"

"Probably because he chose to. But that is beside the point, I suppose. What is it that you want of me?"

"If he asks you, just tell him that there was indeed a man named John Keble."

"He won't believe me any more than he believes you, really."

"Just do it. *Please* Corralie."

Corralie looked at her for a long while, and then at last nodded. "I will do what you ask, Averil."

"Thank you, Corralie." Averil smiled, and for the first time the smile reached her eyes.

"Will you be true to him now?" asked Corralie.

"I think so."

"You only *think* so?"

"I did not know Lawrence could be so—different. It takes a little getting used to."

"But you like him more now?"

"Oh, yes." Averil smiled again. "I like him very much indeed."

"I'm glad, Averil. For both your sakes. Only——" Corralie looked away quickly.

Averil touched her arm. "Madoc? Is that what you are thinking? He didn't love me, I know that. He caught me at a time when—well, when I was miserable because Lawrence was so very gentle all the time. And well, Madoc was a flame and I a very weak moth. There was a time when I could very well have given myself completely to that Welshman of yours. I don't know why he sought me out, and I don't want to know, for I believe it was something I am better knowing nothing about. But I am sorry now for what I threatened yesterday, truly I am."

Corralie nodded wearily. "And so, Averil, am I."

24

Ellen had just finished putting Corralie's hat on the newly pinned curls when Reynold came into the room.

"I've just been in to Chacehampton, Corry."

"Yes?"

"I bumped into Averil."

Corralie nodded at Ellen. "That will be all, thank you, Ellen."

Reynold sniffed and picked up the Chinese box of colors on the dressing table. "Damned expensive paint, this. Yes, as I was saying, I saw Averil. She—er, didn't say a word to me about Vaughan."

"No. She doesn't intend to anymore, for one reason or another."

"Oh, my poor Corry, I'll warrant you could bite your own tongue off."

"Yes." She pulled on her kid riding gloves, stretching and flexing her fingers. "Don't tell Lawrence anything, will you?"

"Hardly. What d'you take me for, girl? It don't change me mind, you know, not one little bit. He's not marrying you."

170

"Why exactly? Because he made up to Averil?"

"Yes."

"And that's the only reason? It's nothing to do with his being virtually penniless by your standards?"

"No—in fact I'd decided to like the fellow last night. But he was making up to Averil *and* to you at the same time. That I won't stand for. If he married you, who's to say he wouldn't carry on where he left off and make up to someone else. Eh?"

"No one, Father. But then, not everyone is so excessively pure-minded as you seem to be."

Reynold cleared his throat, his fingers tapping on the top of the box. "About that other business."

"What other business?"

"The matter of Harry Tindling's movements on Five Warriors' Night."

"Yes?"

"I just wanted to say that I'm still prepared to help Vaughan there."

"How noble."

"Corry, I won't be spoken to in that tone of voice. There is no need for me to help that fellow in any way whatsoever."

"I'm sorry."

"No, you're not—but I'll accept the words at face value. I have reason to believe that Harry does intend sailing that night."

"Oh no——"

"That being the case, I shall have to go to see him, taking Vaughan with me, of course."

"And a pomander?" She looked angrily at him in the mirror. "Or perhaps fleabane?"

Reynold pressed his lips together. "My final word is given on the matter, Corry. You are not going to marry him. As to anything else, I am perfectly prepared to meet him, talk with him, dine with him, or whatever. But he is not marrying you. Is that clear?"

"Perfectly." Her voice was very small. *Oh, damn Lawrence—why could he not have performed his metamorphosis a day earlier?*

"Good. From your toggery, I presume you are going riding?"

"Yes."

"Then you may tell Vaughan that he and I will probably have to see Harry. I take it that you are going to Webley?"

"I was. Yes."

"Just remember——"

"I will remember."

The horizon trembled in the heat as she rode across Bascombe Heath toward the Five Warriors. She maneuvered Pippit around the lumbering ox cart with its load of faggots for the bonfire. Some men were already building the framework in the center of the circle of stones, and they offered their hats to her as she passed.

"Morning, Miss Somerford."

She reined in. "Good morning, Hecky. Shall we have a fine night, then?"

"Ah. No rain around for days to come yet. I feels it in me bones."

"My father is providing three casks for the junketings this year."

The man's eyes gleamed and he grinned, revealing his uneven teeth. "Aw, 'twill be a powerful night, right enough. Mind, half the menfolk of Chacehampton won't be there with us, but that can't be helped."

"The *Laura?*"

"Ah—Harry says as he can't afford to leave her idle for another full moon, not after her being laid up for so long."

"I suppose not." She looked across toward Selney Bill and the *Janus*.

Hecky followed her gaze. "Ah—that there sloop's a pest, mind. 'Special as 'er's got that watch up on the head."

"I didn't think Harry would risk going out under the circumstances."

"Can't afford not to, like I said. Anyway, we could sit tight for a year and that there sloop might do the same. We'd be in a poor way then, wouldn't we?" He spat on his hands to ease the blisters there. "Stackin' them barrels th'other night gived me 'ell. You—er, you goin' down Webley then, Miss Corralie?"

"Yes."

"That there Welshman—he'm all right, I suppose. I knows as Harry let him go an' all, but he saw our faces——"

"He's all right, I promise you."

"I wondered like, what with him suddenly coming here. A swell like that can't be 'ere for th'air, can he?"

"He has his reasons, Hecky."

He grinned then. "Ah, reckon us'll be having two grand matches to celebrate soon, eh?"

She smiled and looked at Pippit's mane. "Well, one anyway. Good day to you, Hecky."

"Good day, Miss Corralie."

Madoc lifted her down from the saddle and kissed her. "I was coming to call upon you this afternoon."

"Oh, Madoc——" She hid her face against his shoulder and burst into tears.

"What is it? Tell me." He put his hand to her chin and lifted her face gently.

"My father will not let me marry you."

"Because I am chasing his fortune?"

"No."

"Why then?" He stroked her cheek softly.

"Because of Averil."

"Averil? But how——? *She* told him?"

"No. Oh, Madoc, if I hadn't been so stupid, everything would be all right still. You see, she threatened that she would tell him, because she said you'd made her look foolish. But then she changed her mind and I didn't know. I told my father, thinking—— Oh, I don't know anymore what I was thinking when I did it."

He pulled her close. "Don't cry."

"I can't help it—he's so, so *determined* about it."

"Would you marry me, anyway? Without his consent?"

"He'd disinherit me."

He smiled. "So. We'd have to manage some other way, wouldn't we?"

She raised her head. "Do you mean that?"

"Of course I mean it. Sweet Lord, Corry, I want you before I want your money—which I never thought would be the case for Madoc Vaughan's fine ambitions. But nonetheless, it is so." He kissed her. "After all this, when Catti and Charles are together again, will you come away with me? I can make you a titled if impoverished lady."

She nodded. "I will."

He led her across the courtyard and into the garden. "Only two days to go, Corry, and then, pray God, Charles will be landed safely."

"The *Laura* is sailing."

"No Five Warriors' Night for our good friend, eh?"

"No."

"That means the chance of the *Janus* sailing as well. Damn it all; it will be like Hyde Park out there."

"My father says that he will go to see Harry with you."

"He can stomach doing that still?"

"Yes. He said he would, and he will stand by that."

"I will come at any time he appoints."

She turned to him. "Oh, Madoc, I do love you so. But it seems that everything is determined to—to make our lives difficult."

"Ah, but true love conquers all. So I'm told." He kissed her again.

25

The landau halted at the end of the quay, its long evening shadow falling across the *Fair Maid* as she rocked gently on the swell.

Corralie waited as her father alighted. "I'm coming in with you, Father."

"I suppose that having come thus far you may as well come in. But don't interfere. Isn't that Vaughan's nag?" He pointed to where The Beau was tethered to a fence.

"Yes. Yes, and there's Madoc."

He came slowly toward them, an elegant figure in his dark green coat and lace-trimmed shirt. His cravat fluttered in the strong sea breeze as he removed his top hat and bowed to them.

"Good evening, Corry." He inclined his head to Reynold.

Reynold returned the salute in an equally stiff manner. "I trust that Tindling has no notion of your dalliance with his daughter."

"None at all."

"Then let us proceed. Corry? My arm, if you please." Reynold held out his arm.

They walked up the path toward the rambling

old house, and Corralie could smell the perfume of the pinks that grew on either side of the path. In the latticed porch sat a large tabby cat with unblinking amber eyes. Reynold knocked upon the peeling, white-painted door.

Averil opened it, her eyes widening at first as she saw Madoc. Her glance flew to Corralie and Reynold. "Yes?"

Reynold nodded. "Your father expects us, Averil."

"Oh, Oh, yes." She stepped aside, keeping her eyes averted from Madoc.

Harry sat in the kitchen, a mug of strong ale on the scrubbed table beside him. His stockinged feet were stretched out toward the range. Behind him a dresser filled the one white-washed wall, with blue and white crockery hanging from its hooks. A ship's bell stood in the corner. Madoc bowed his head beneath the low door, and his hessians sounded loud on the red-tiled floor.

Harry looked at him in surprise and then at Reynold. "I thought as it were just between you and me, Mr. Somerford."

"So it is, indirectly. I've a favor to ask of you, Harry."

"Ah!"

Reynold pushed another cat from the settle and sat down. "Damned cats everywhere here, Harry! No one's got that many rodents."

"I like cats. Damme if I didn't marry one, anyway!" Harry threw back his head and laughed uproariously. "Her name were Tabitha, an' all."

"Harry, I believe you're taking the *Laura* out tomorrow night."

Harry's smile faded. "That's not information to toss around in company, Mr. Somerford."

"It's important, Harry. And I mean that in all sincerity."

"Then—yes, she'm going out at high tide tomorrow evening. Navy or no navy."

"Harry, would you be prepared to hold back sailing once more?"

"Why?"

"To keep the *Janus* safely where she is."

"Why?"

"Because there is a ship coming into Webley Bay tomorrow night and the last thing we want is for the *Janus* to be nosing about. If you stay in, then most probably Chadwick will let his men ashore for the celebration."

"And this 'ere 'other ship' can come and go peaceable, eh?"

"Yes, that is the general idea."

"Who is she, then?"

"A lugger. From the Mediterranean. She's putting a man ashore at Webley—Sir Madoc's brother-in-law. It's very important, Harry—the fellow's bringing word of a plot to kill Bonaparte."

Harry stared at Reynold and then his sandy eyes slid to Madoc and Corralie. "Kill Bonaparte?"

"Yes."

"Well, now, that'd be a real shame, wouldn't it? I drinks a toast to Boney most nights—beggin' him to get hisself off've his back end again and bring some money back into my line of business." Harry grinned broadly. "He'm good for trade. So, Vaughan, your brother-in-law's got word to stop this plan Mister Somerford has mentioned?"

"Yes."

"Keeping the *Laura* in will cost a pretty penny."

Madoc took a long breath. "How much?"

"The price of two and a half thousand casks of cognac."

Corralie sat forward. "We'll pay you, Harry, have no fear."

Reynold scowled. "What with?" he snapped.

She raised her chin. "My jewels."

"They're not yours to give away!"

"Oh yes, they are——they were left to me by Mother. And I choose to offer them to Harry for his trouble."

Harry's eyes glittered. "That mean that diamond choker as you wore once to that reception in the Town Hall?"

"Yes."

Madoc put his hand over hers. "You can't pay for this, Corry—after all it's none of your problem."

She smiled. "I will use my jewels. For Catti's sake. Now, there is nothing you can argue about there, is there?"

He nodded slightly. "No—it is unarguable, I suppose."

Harry snapped his fingers at Averil. "Bring that flagon here, missy. That's right. Now then, Sir Madoc. This 'ere lugger, who is she?"

"A *chasse-marée*. Three masts."

The ale glugged into the mug. "Three-masted French lugger, eh? Decked-in?"

"Er—yes. I believe so."

Again the sandy eyes were glittering, and Corralie felt suddenly uneasy. Harry wiped a drip of ale from the table with a dirty thumb. "There ain't many of them about. *Belle Marie*, is it?" His eyes did not waver from Corralie's face, and he was rewarded immediately by the widening of her eyes. He sat back and exhaled slowly. "Darnier. In my neck of the woods."

Madoc leaned back against the dresser. "He's not coming on any competitive business. He's just dropping my brother-in-law and taking himself away again."

"It's still Darnier."

Corralie swallowed. "Harry, if we offer you

morc, will you keep the *Laura* in tomorrow
night?"

"How much more?"

"Twice the value of your two and a half thousand casks."

"Corry!" Madoc put his hand on her shoulder.

Harry nodded. "'Tis a deal then, Miss Corralie.
For twice my cargo's value I will keep the *Laura* in
tomorrow night. She'll not be leaving her moorings."

Reynold stood. "Your hand on it, Harry."

Harry reached across the table and took the old
man's bony hand. "I usually spits on a deal, Mister
Somerford, but seeing as it's you——"

"Good night, Harry."

"Good night, Miss Corralie. Gentlemen."

When they had gone, Averil came back into the
kitchen. "What are you up to?"

"Keep your educated nose out, Averil."

"But you gave your word."

"And I shall keep it, don't you fret." He grinned.
"That 'Zekiel still out the back?"

"Yes."

"Send him on in, then—go on, wench. I knows as
you're out of the habit of doing as you're told by
the likes of me, but until you've got Kendal to the
altar you're still my daughter."

"I'm not likely to forget that."

The mug thumped onto the table and he caught
her wrist. "I made you what you are now, missy,
and don't you forget it. I put money out on you
when you went to that fancy school, and had me
leg pulled by those around here as thought it was
getting meself up above me station. But when you
walks down the aisle on Kendal's arm, they'll laugh
t'other sides of their faces. You're Harry Tindling's
daughter, and you'll take a grand dowry to Kendal.
And you'll be Lady Kendal. But underneath, you'll

still have come from this house and this background. So don't you go looking down your nose at it or at me. D'you hear me?"

"Yes, Father."

"Right. Get 'Zekiel in here, then."

26

The sunset on Five Warriors' Night was as fine as any Corralie had ever seen. She rode Pippit toward the standing stones where the huge bonfire stood waiting and where a crowd was already gathering. Someone was playing a fiddle to the thumping accompaniment of a drum, and a little dog with a ridiculous skirt on was dancing and yapping at the same time. Beyond the fallen stone, some men were shouting and arguing about fighting cocks which fluttered and squawked on the ground, arching their necks and flying at each other with their sharp claws.

Corralie turned in the saddle to look out to sea, where there was not a sail to be seen. The fortifications on Selney Bill showed clearly against the scarlet water, and the *Janus* looked so small at her moorings.

A pieman wandered through the crowd ringing his handbell and calling his wares. "Pies! Hot pies! Best mutton!"

Down in Chacehampton the procession was just leaving the outskirts of the town, with bobbing lanterns and a lot of merry shouting and singing. Corralie watched them until the woods at the foot of the heath hid them from sight.

It wasn't high tide for another hour yet—— She moved Pippit on past the crowds and down the heath toward Webley. In the twilight, she didn't see 'Zekiel at first. It was his horse that gave him away. It caught Pippit's scent and called out. Corralie reined in, straining to look through the half light.

" 'Zekiel?" She could make out his dumpy figure on the horse by the gorse bush.

"Miss Corralie." He cleared his throat uncomfortably.

"Whatever are you doing so far from the junketings?"

"Waiting for someone."

His tone precluded any further probing, but as she rode on she felt uneasy, in the same way she had with Harry Tindling the night before. As she reached the trees of Bascombe Woods she halted her mount again and turned to look back up the heath. 'Zekiel's silhouette was plain against the skyline. As she looked, she saw the flash of the dying sun on the telescope he was looking through. Her breath caught in her throat. He was looking out to sea; and he was Harry Tindling's man.

Catti shivered at the open window. It was completely dark now, and the sounds of the people on the heath drifted on the breeze. Charles's portrait looked monotone in the darkness, and Catti glanced at it. "Pray God all is well this time——"

Madoc smiled. "We'll soon know now."

"Is it high tide?"

"Ten minutes ago." He put his arm around Corralie. "You are sure Tindling's man is watching?"

"As sure as anyone can be, and he wasn't too pleased that I saw him."

"What's Tindling up to, then? He gave his word. But could he maneuver around it somehow? He said the *Laura* wouldn't sail tonight."

"He hasn't got anything else comparable, Madoc, and certainly nothing else that is armed."

He looked at her suddenly. "There's the *Janus*."

"He'd set the *Janus* on Darnier?" she gasped.

Catti's voice came excitedly from the window. "Madoc, there's a ship signaling far out. Three long and one short. Three long and one short."

He opened his telescope and trained it on the sea. "Yes, it's the *Belle Marie!* I can make out her one red sail now."

"Shall I light the lantern, Madoc?" Catti's voice was trembling so much that it was scarcely more than a husky whisper.

"Yes, *cariad*."

Taking Corralie's hand, Madoc led her along the dusty passageway until they came to a window that looked up toward the heath. The bonfire burned brightly, smoke and sparks flying into the sky. He put the telescope to his eye again, searching the heath for the gorse bush Corralie had spoken of. And then saw 'Zekiel's figure, a mere shadow against the skyline. As he watched, the man gathered his reins and turned his horse to ride swiftly past the bonfire and the crowds and down the heath toward Chacehampton.

Corralie stood beside him. "Do you see anything?"

"Yes. Our friend is riding back toward the town. It must be the *Belle Marie* he's watching for, then. He's gone before she's close enough to identify, unless you know exactly what you're looking for." He smiled ruefully. "Let's get down to the beach. There's nothing we can do about it except hope that Darnier at least manages to land Charles."

"If Charles is with him."

"Aye—if Charles is with him."

Harry looked up as 'Zekiel opened the door. "Well?"

"She'm coming. Three-masted lugger. One red sail. That the one?"

"That's her. Right, 'Zekiel. You've got some rowing to do, now. Get that there bit of paper out to the *Janus*. Say as you was paid by a stranger to give it into Chadwick's lily-white hands. Right?" Harry filled his mug again. "But mind, now. Give Darnier time to drop his precious cargo. We do want the plan to snuff Boney to be snuffed itself, don't we?"

"She'll be half an hour tacking into Webley in this wind."

"Give her half an hour then, my lad. Oh, and 'Zekiel—that there Robbo should be outside waiting. Tell him as he's to get as many of the lads together as he can. We've got a little trip to make to Webley. I knows that Darnier scum. He'll not trust anyone else to collect his payment; he'll drop his cargo in person. And I wants him."

"Yes, Harry." 'Zekiel picked up the piece of folded paper and went out again.

The time on the beach seemed without end as they waited for the lugger to tack across the entrance of the bay. Her bow dipped and rose as the cross currents caught her and her sails strained as she came slowly past the rocks, which were hardly visible at high tide and were therefore so very dangerous.

Catti stood quietly, staring at the lugger, and her lips moved silently as if she were praying.

The boat was lowered and they distinctly heard the winches on the lugger above the noise of the waves on the beach.

"How many are getting in her, Madoc?" Catti caught his arm.

He lowered the telescope again. "Two."

Chadwick stood with his hands behind his back, looking at 'Zekiel. "You have a message for me?"

"Yes, sir." He handed the paper to the captain.

Chadwick read it and then gave it to Lieutenant Hughes. "Honor among thieves, eh, lieutenant?"

"Shall you follow it up?"

"One smuggler is as good as another. It may not be the *Laura*, but it will do for the moment. Order all hands at the ready, lieutenant."

"Yes, sir."

Chadwick looked at 'Zekiel. "Tell your master that his turn will come."

"I was given the note by a stranger, sir."

"Really. Get him off this ship—he smells worse than a slaver."

The rowing boat made very slow headway through the choppy waves, and to those waiting on the beach it seemed that they had been watching her for the best part of an hour.

"Is it Charles? Can you see?"

"Catti, that thing is bobbing like a corkscrew—I can't make anything out properly."

Corralie's heart was thundering with excitement and fear. She looked behind at the heath where the bonfire was flaring higher now, its flames fanned by the breeze. A tall column of smoke and sparks drifted seaward, and the smell of burning pricked her nostrils.

The rowing boat was nearer now and they could hear the oars in the rowlocks. Madoc raised the telescope yet again. "It's Charles! Catti, he's there!"

She ran to the water's edge, the waves creaming

and frothing around her ankles and her shawl fluttering. "Charles!"

"Catherine!"

Corralie gripped Madoc's arm. "It's going to be all right——"

But she spoke too soon. The sloop's crisp white sails moved smoothly around the headland, the ensigns streaming from her masts. The *Janus* fired a warning cannon across the lugger's bows.

"Sweet God!" whispered Madoc, and Catti's excited figure was suddenly still as she watched.

Aboard the *Belle Marie*, they had already seen the danger even before the cannon was fired and the anchor was being weighed. The lugger's bows turned, her sails hoisting swiftly as she came around with the wind behind her.

The wind was against the *Janus*, but still the gap between her and the lugger's escape was narrowing with each second. The *Belle Marie* moved sharply, carrying as much sail as she could to gain the benefit of the following wind, and Corralie held her breath as the sleek French craft slipped from the mouth of the bay right beneath the very bows of the sloop. Chadwick's ship maneuvered to turn in time, and those on the shore distinctly heard an ominous grating sound from the sloop as she touched on the submerged rocks. But she seemed unharmed as she came around in the wake of her prey.

The rowing boat nudged ashore and Charles jumped out, catching Catti in his arms and holding her tight, his eyes closed. He looked so different in ordinary clothes, thought Corralie, who had pictured him only in the uniform he wore in his portrait.

Darnier leaped ashore, standing there watching his ship's flight and then turning to look at Madoc.

"A Swedish tub, you said, *monsieur*—so much for an Englishman's word!"

"You have Tindling to thank for this, Darnier."

"Listen!" Corralie held up her hand. "Listen, someone's calling!"

They all turned as a voice drifted on the wind again. "Madoc!"

Corralie looked at him. "It's Averil's voice, I'm sure of it." As she spoke, they saw Averil and Lawrence at the top of the cliff.

Lawrence waved his arm urgently. "Vaughan? Come quickly!"

Averil's face was tear-stained, and she clung to Lawrence's arm. "It's my father! You'll have to be quick!"

"Why?" asked Madoc quickly.

"My father knows that Darnier will come ashore in person, and he's getting his men together to find him."

Darnier crossed himself and looked faint.

"My father told 'Zekiel to take word to the *Janus* and then to have his men gathered to come out here. I overheard him when I was waiting for Lawrence to take me to the heath."

"How much time have we got, Averil?"

"Ten minutes. No more," said Lawrence, looking then at Darnier. "Where can we hide him? There isn't an inch of this country that Harry doesn't know like the back of his hand."

Madoc sighed. "Kendal, I haven't the faintest clue. Not the faintest."

Lawrence smiled, then. "I have my landau in the courtyard. There's still a good tide running—the *Fair Maid* is seaworthy again. She could catch the *Belle Marie*. Chadwick won't give chase for long, not if that noise I heard was anything to go by.

That *chasse-marée* can outrun most things, but not my cutter."

Madoc grinned then. "I knew the Almighty had some great destiny in mind for you, Kendal!"

"I have my moments. Get him into the landau, then."

Darnier shook his head. "Not without my payment. I delivered Beauchamp and must be paid. I cannot go back to my ship without it."

Madoc pushed a purse into his hands. "Here it is, in full."

The Frenchman snatched it and then nodded curtly to Lawrence. "I am yours, *monsieur*."

"God forbid," murmured Lawrence, but he looked at Madoc again. "Far be it from me to alarm you still further, Vaughan, but Chadwick was rather thorough, I fear. He sent a man ashore to the fort at Cannutbury. I believe you will be overrun by the army shortly, searching for anyone or anything that may have been put ashore illegally by the French smuggler. I doubt that they will ask questions first, if you take my meaning."

Catti hid her face against Charles's chest. "No! Please, no——"

Darnier was concerned only with his own situation, and he shook Lawrence's arm. "The tide will not wait, even for you, *milord*!"

Madoc turned to Charles. "Perhaps the *Fair Maid* would be your best hope, too, under the circumstances."

"No, my friend. I stay here now and take my chance."

Lawrence nodded and turned toward the gateway into the courtyard, but Averil went with him. "Averil, it would be better for you to stay here."

"I will come with you, Lawrence," she said softly, "You'll not go anywhere without me now."

Madoc watched them go and then turned helplessly to Charles. "I don't know where to hide you. They'll go through everything here with a fine-tooth comb."

Corralie took his hands. "They wouldn't search Somerford Place."

"Corry, your father wouldn't have it——"

"He won't know, will he? He's up at the junket-ings on Bascombe Heath I think, and if I know him, he'll stay until the bitter end. I'll take Charles and we'll go up over the heath past the crowds. We'll hardly be noticed that way. Then there are back lanes to the house."

"I'll come, too."

"No, someone must stay with poor Catti. Just get a good horse for Charles."

The Beau danced around, swishing his tail nervously, as Madoc tightened the girths.

"Stick with Corry, Charles, and don't say anything to anyone—no one will believe *you* are a Dorset man!" He handed over the reins.

Charles kissed Catti again and mounted the horse. "You know, Madoc, my friend, it was all in vain. All of this. Bonaparte did not trust me in the end—any plans he may have are unknown to me. My handsome hide nearly decorated his villa walls. But it was worth the try, eh?"

Madoc nodded. "It was worth the try."

Catti watched them ride away beneath the gateway, the hooves thundering momentarily on the old wood of the drawbridge and then sounding more and more distant as they moved toward the shelter of Bascombe Woods. She slipped her hand in Madoc's, her eyes full of tears.

"Well, at least he is safe in England again, even if it all came to nothing."

He squeezed her fingers. "I pray God England *is* safe, Catti."

"Corry was right, you know. They won't search her father's house."

"I hope not, for if anything should happen to her——"

"You love her a lot, don't you, Madoc?"

"More than my life, *cariad*, more than my life."

27

The bonfire's crackling was almost frightening as Corralie and Charles mingled with the crowds of laughing, shouting people. The full moon shone brightly over the sea and several of the crowd were still watching the sloop and the lugger out on the silver water, but most had returned to the enjoyment of Five Warriors' Night.

Corralie caught Charles's hand and pointed down at Chacehampton harbor. "There goes the *Fair Maid*. See?" They watched as the low-slung racing cutter slipped from the narrow harbor entrance and out into the bay. Her main sail was hoisted and even from that distance they could see the sudden surge forward she made as the wind caught her.

Charles smiled at her. "Well, one of us at least has got away. But, *mademoiselle*, I have not the pleasure of knowing your name, a sad thing when you are so instrumental in helping me."

She looked at his thin, good-looking face, liking him immensely. "My name is Corralie Somerford."

He raised her hand to his lips, but at that moment she saw her father and Lady Agnes. They stood by the bonfire, laughing as the hobbyhorse leaped wildly to and fro. Her father was the last person she wished to see at this moment. She held his hand urgently. "My father is over there. Let us put the bonfire between us and him, shall we?"

"If that is your wish." They turned quickly, for at that moment they heard another sound, that of many horses galloping along the bottom road toward Webley. "Your army, I believe, *mademoiselle*. They—they will not harm Catherine? Or Madoc?"

"No. It is a French smuggler they are looking for, isn't it?"

She moved on, leading Pippit through the crowds to the other side of the bonfire. The procession was encircling the flames, chanting monotonously as the man playing the part of the unfortunate king was drummed ahead of them with his hobbyhorse steed.

> *It's Warrior Night tonight*
> *Give us a candle, give us a light*
> *If you don't, you'll get a fright——*

And with the last word the leaders of the procession closed in on the king and stamped their feet. The king's hobbyhorse capered around him, its blue-and-red checkered caparison flashing with silvered threads as it skipped, jaws snapping at any unwary person in the laughing crowd.

"Miss Corralie?"

Corralie turned sharply and saw Ellen. "You gave me a start!"

"I thought it was you, miss——" The maid's eyes went curiously to Charles, and then she smiled at Corralie again. "That's my Danny being the hobby."

"Danny the Reluctant Lover?"

"Yes, Miss Corralie." Ellen flushed and lowered her eyes. "Reckon I'll get him to the church yet."

"It won't be for lack of trying, will it?" Corralie spoke as casually as she could, linking her arm through Charles's and behaving as if she had known him for a long time.

"Did you see the sloop chasing that lugger, Miss Corralie?"

"Yes."

"She won't catch her, Danny said as much."

"Danny has time to notice such things when he is busy transporting his king to the stones?"

"Oh, we have to rest now and then, miss, you know that. He'll have to sit down again in a moment—they've been around that fire that many times now I can hardly believe they haven't fallen in a faint!" Ellen laughed, but then her smile faded. "Look, Miss Corralie, isn't that the soldiers from the fort over by Cannutbury?"

Corralie and Charles turned quickly and saw the soldiers emerging from the woods behind them, fanning out in a long line and walking slowly toward the crowds.

"*Dieu!* They have guessed——!" Charles turned to mount The Beau, but Corralie held his arm.

"No, that would give the game away completely if we fled now!"

Ellen stared at her mistress and then at Charles. "Miss Corralie?"

"Ellen—your Danny, would he help us?" Corralie glanced at the hobbyhorse, which had collapsed at last beside the bonfire to the accompaniment of jeers and good-natured laughter. The king sat down wearily beside his steed, his ridiculously large and ornate crown falling forward over his face.

"Help you, Miss Corralie? How?"

"By changing places with my friend here?"

"Oh, I don't know, Miss Corralie. If the army are searching for him——"

"They aren't. They are searching for smugglers."

Ellen searched her face anxiously. "I believe you, Miss Corralie. I'll go and fetch Danny now."

Charles smiled. "Bless you, *mademoïselle*."

Danny shuffled awkwardly across the heath toward them, his cumbersome horse costume flapping in the strong breeze. He looked vaguely funny, his round country face peering through the opening in the horse's neck. "Aw, I don't know, Ellen—I'm that tired now——" he was grumbling as she dragged him in front of Corralie.

"Hold your tongue, Danny Juro and do as you're told. Here he is, Miss Corralie."

"Danny? Will you help us?" Corralie glanced behind at the soldiers, who were so much nearer now. The smoke from the fire drifted over the scene, obscuring everything for a moment.

"Ellen says as I must get out of Hobby."

"Please."

He looked back at his companions, who were busy opening one of Reynold's casks, still laughing and joking together and not noticing the horse's absence. The fiddle and the drum played more scratchily than ever, and the soldiers had hardly been noticed yet.

"I don't know." Danny looked worried, " 'Tis only once as a man gets to be Hobby."

Corralie pleaded. "Please, Danny, it's so very important and it will be only for a short while, until——"

He followed her glance. "Until the army's finished searching?"

"Yes."

He nodded then. "All right, Miss Somerford, I'll do as you ask."

"Thank you, Danny."

He wriggled out of the costume and pushed it into Corralie's hands. "I don't want to see any more, Miss Somerford, for reckon if I don't know I can't be blamed, can I?"

"No."

"You just call me when you wants me. That's all."

Charles raised his eyebrows as he lifted the horse from the ground. "So great a downfall for an aide-de-camp?"

"Nonsense—you are about to become a king's favorite steed, what more could you want?" She smiled as she pulled the caparison over his head. "Go on, then; they've begun the dance again. Well, go on—all you've got to do is caper around and snap at the crowds. There, with that little string. That's right, you're snapping very well. Hurry." She gave him a little push.

He lumbered through the crowds, dutifully snapping and lunging from side to side, and was rewarded by the instant squeals and giggles as people dodged away from him. Corralie watched him for a moment and then turned to looked at the soldiers, who were on the rim of the crowd now.

Ellen moved closer to her mistress. "Who is he, Miss Corralie?"

"Lady Catherine's husband."

"Why do they search for him?"

"They know that someone came ashore from that lugger the *Janus* was pursuing." She smiled. "At least, they're searching for anyone who *may* have been put ashore."

Ellen took The Beau's reins from her. "Someone had better look as if they have brought this horse here, then—he's too grand to be just anyone's. Look, there's Gerry. Gerry?" Before Corralie had time to say anything, the maid was calling the groom from Somerford Place who was busily engaged in consuming a steaming hot mutton pie.

Reluctantly he came across the heath. "You wanted me, Miss Corralie?"

"Yes. Here, look after him for me." She pushed The Beau's reins into the astonished man's hands. "You are riding him because you have to be back at Somerford Place before midnight to attend a sick mare."

"Eh? But 'tis my night off——"

"Gerry, just say what I've told you to say if anyone asks you about the horse. All right?" Corralie glared at him.

He swallowed the last of the pie. "Yes, Miss Corralie."

A sergeant was close by, asking the parson some questions, and the parson was shaking his balding head. Corralie held her breath, for she knew instinctively that the next on the sergeant's list was herself, and sure enough he came toward her, saluting smartly.

"Miss Somerford, isn't it?"

"Yes, sergeant."

"I'm sorry to trouble you, Miss Somerford, but have you seen any strangers here tonight?"

"Sergeant, it's such a crowd I could have seen a hundred strangers and not realized it."

"You've noticed no one, then?"

"No."

He glanced at The Beau and then at Gerry. "A fine horse, that."

Gerry's eyes widened. "It ain't mine! I works for Mr. Somerford."

"Let you ride his horses any time, does he?"

"No! I've to be back at midnight, there's a sick mare to see to then. Miss Corralie said as I was to have a good horse to get me back quickly."

The sergeant looked at Corralie again. "That so, Miss Somerford?"

"Yes."

"I'm sorry to have troubled you, Miss Somerford, but if you should see anyone——"

"I will be sure to inform you should I do so, sergeant."

He saluted again and moved on through the crowds.

Gerry's eyes were still like saucers. "Did I do all right, Miss Corralie?"

"Yes. Yes, of course you did. Thank you. And thank *you*, Ellen."

The maid smiled. "You wouldn't have thought of the horse, would you?"

"No."

"I've courted Danny long enough to know that he's one of Harry Tindling's men and to know too what's looked for in a search like they're doing now. It's odd things like horses that often do the damage."

"I begin to wonder if there is anyone in Chacehampton who isn't part of Harry Tindling's enterprise. Have they gone yet? I can't see."

Ellen turned, peering through the swirling smoke. "Yes—yes, I can see them going on down toward Chacehampton. Here's Hobby come back to us."

Charles lifted the costume over his head and sighed with relief. "I did not think we would get away with that, *mademoiselle*. I must thank you—er, Danny." He gave the horse into Danny's hand as the young man rejoined them.

Danny looked at him. "You're a froggie, ain't you?"

Charles inclined his head warily. Danny looked at Corralie. "Most of our lot's gone looking for Darnier of the *Belle Marie*. I stayed only on account of I was Hobby this year. Miss Corralie, is this here Darnier?"

"No. I swear not, Danny. Harry will have no cause to punish you for helping us."

Danny nodded. "Reckon that's that, then. Come on, Ellen. They've started the dance again. All right, all right, I'm coming, give us a chance——" He was grumbling as he pulled Hobby over his head and hurried to rejoin his shouting companions.

Charles took The Beau's reins from Gerry. "Where now, *mademoiselle?*"

"Somerford Place. Follow me." She mounted and turned Pippit away from the bonfire.

As the horses moved slowly forward, Ellen suddenly hurried across the crowded heath to catch Pippit's bridle.

"Miss Corralie! The soldiers were heard saying that they were going to search the whole of Chacehampton. House by house. They know it was the *Belle Marie* and that Mister Darnier is wanted for a good deal."

Corralie's heart fell. A house by house search——

Charles looked at her. "Perhaps it would be better to go back to Webley."

"No, they will have left guards there. No—I still think Somerford Place is the best place. Come on."

28

Somerford Place seemed quiet. The stable yard was deserted as Corralie and Charles put the two horses into empty stalls and closed the doors. She stood, listening. The glow of the bonfire lit up the sky above Bascombe Heath, but from this distance they could hear nothing. The strong wind bent the trees beyond the outbuildings and rippled the surfaces of the lakes, throwing the spray of the fountains over the path as they hurried toward the house.

The door into the buttery was unlocked, and its latch made little sound as Corralie pushed it gently open. The shelves and red-raddled tiles of the echoing room were quite clear in the moonlight as the door swung.

Charles caught her arm. "You leave your house unattended like this?"

"No, there are servants here somewhere—I just would like to pass them without their knowing you are here."

"They are not loyal?"

"Oh, yes——but they are also friends of Harry Tindling's, and they may imagine you to be Darnier. Everything is best if they remain in ignorance, don't you think?"

He nodded.

By the laundry rooms they stopped again, for the low murmur of voices could be heard in the main kitchen and occasional bursts of raucous laughter.

"They're playing cards in there." She put her finger to her lips and took his hand, leading him slowly along the low, white-washed passage. Through the half-open door of the kitchen they could see the card players. They sat around the huge scrubbed table, their faces lit by an oil lamp. One of the maids stood with her arms around a footman's neck, her chin resting on the top of his head as she surveyed his hand. He lifted his face and she dropped a kiss on his lips for luck.

Corralie drew Charles quickly past the doorway and on by the pantries toward the steps leading up into the main house. It was strange and unreal to be scurrying like a thief through one's own home.

The hallway seemed quiet as they slowly ascended into the bright, chandelier-lit area where the air was sweet with the perfume of roses from the vases on the low tables. As they appeared at the top of the steps, Haines sat up in surprise, the week-old copy of the *Times* falling from his lap.

"Miss Corralie?" He tugged his crooked periwig forward into place and straightened his cravat.

"Haines!" She felt foolish. "I did not think you would be here."

"I cannot read when the others are playing cards, Miss Corralie. The noise, you understand." The butler's eyes went to Charles as he got to his feet.

"Haines, I must trust you now."

"You may always trust me, Miss Corralie," he said with some dignity.

She glanced back down the steps as another roar

of laughter emanated from the kitchens. "Haines, you have not seen anyone else apart from myself."

"No, Miss Corralie."

"Thank you, Haines."

"Not at all, Miss Corralie."

"Have you the key to the attic stairs?"

"It is down in the kitchens on the hook."

"Then bring it, if you please."

He bowed and went past them toward the basement.

Charles smiled at her. "An attic refuge, *mademoiselle?*"

"No one ever goes up there—except my father when he decides to search for something he put there years ago."

"And for how long do you think your army will look?"

"I don't know."

He took her hand and raised it to his lips. "*Mademoiselle*, I thank you now for what you are doing. You—you are betrothed to my friend Madoc?"

She looked away. "Not exactly."

"Oh, forgive me—I thought——"

"You thought correctly, *monsieur*, but there are—obstacles."

Haines returned with the bunch of keys and a lamp, and they followed him up the wide stairs.

At the top of the house, the butler put the key in the lock and turned it with some difficulty. As he stood aside for them to go up the uncarpeted steps to the attic rooms, she turned to him. "Haines, I think a tray of supper would not go amiss. You may say that I have returned early and that I wish to eat."

"Yes, Miss Corralie." He bowed, handing Charles the lamp and then walking away.

The attics smelled musty and damp, even though

the summer had warmed the still air beneath the roof. Old, forgotten things littered the rooms, gathering dust and cobwebs. Corralie smiled as she saw her old dolls lying on a shelf, and her rocking horse with his once red bridle hanging broken. Charles looked around and then at her.

"Attics, *mademoiselle*, know no national barriers, do they? There was just such a clutter at my own home in France."

"Will you return there with Catti?"

He shrugged with Gallic expressiveness. "Who can say? If the state of peace between our nations remains, then yes. But if the Emperor rises again——"

"Will he?"

"Yes. Oh, I have no proof, but I know it. Here." He put his hand against his heart. "Elba is not sufficient for the man who once ruled most of Europe."

"And if he has such a plan, he did not include you in it?"

"No." He smiled then, pushing an old rug from the top of a chest and sitting down. "My English-Welsh wife made me a doubtful prospect. And when I sought to learn anything by other means, my activities aroused suspicion. I barely escaped his guards, and had it not been for friends in Portoferraio, I would not be here now. As it was, I missed the *Belle Marie* the first time. I knew she was there, waiting for me, but I could not leave my hiding place."

"But in the end you got away?"

"Yes. The sting had gone from the search by then and I think the Emperor thought I had managed to leave Elba already. So, two weeks before full moon, I made my way to the *rendezvous* and was waiting when the *Belle Marie* entered the bay. And here I am—straight from one crisis into another."

"It is only because of rivalry between two scoundrels."

"Darnier met his match tonight, did he not?" Charles leaned his head wearily against the wall.

She turned as Haines came up the steps, a candle flickering on the tray he carried. He set it down next to Charles.

"I brought some blue vinney, some good crusty bread and a bottle of Medoc, Miss Corralie. And some of the cook's best Madeira cake. Will that be enough—oh, and some cold roast beef."

Charles nodded at him. "That will be excellent. *Merci.*"

Haines's eyes widened as he heard the unmistakable accent. "Miss Corralie, one of the maids has returned from the heath. She said that the soldiers are searching for a Frenchman——"

"They are, Haines, but not this particular Frenchman, I promise you."

"Yes, Miss Corralie."

As he finished speaking, a new sound carried through the attic windows—the sound of many horses coming up the long drive. Corralie flew to the grimy window, wiping it with her handkerchief to look out. "It's the soldiers, I can make out their red coats!"

Haines turned. "I will go down, Miss Corralie."

"Haines——?"

"Do not worry, Miss Corralie." The butler bowed proudly.

The sergeant took off his gloves and looked around the elegant hall. "No one in, you say?"

"Only Miss Somerford, and she is asleep in her bed."

"She was at the heath, wasn't she?"

"I believe so." Haines looked down his long nose at the soldier.

"Came back early, did she?"

"So it would appear. She was feeling unwell."

"So—there's no one else come here?"

"I am not in the habit of letting anyone into this house!"

"Well, I'll just have a word with the rest of the servants, if you don't mind."

"The entrance to the basements is at the back of the house."

"And the stairs down to them are just across this hall."

"Only guests and gentry enter the house through this door. If you wish to speak with the servants, then you must use the correct entrance."

The sergeant glared at him. "Damned fool way of going about it!"

"Nevertheless—I shall await you at the back entrance." Haines closed the doors in the sergeant's face.

He took a long breath, looking up the main stairs as he crossed the hall. His footsteps sounded loud as he went down to the rooms below.

The card game came to an abrupt halt as the soldiers hammered on the door of the buttery.

The sergeant walked in without waiting and looked around the sea of startled faces. "So—you don't all get to go to the junketings, eh?"

Haines cleared his throat. "The house cannot be left unattended—we drew lots and the luckier ones went to the heath."

The sergeant's eyes went over the room. "Anyone been here tonight?" His eyes stopped on the cook's round face.

"No," she said, her eyes round. "No one's been here—'ceptin' Miss Corralie. Did her some supper on a tray, I did. There's been no one else."

The sergeant nodded. "Right, but then anyone

could come in through the hallowed main doors and you wouldn't know, would you?"

"Well—no, but then Mister Haines would have to open the main door and he says that Miss Corralie came back. That's all." The cook smoothed her starched apron nervously.

"Yes." The sergeant looked with dislike at the butler. "Reckon I've got to search the house, Mister Haines."

"Not without Miss Corralie's permission. And she's asleep in her bed."

"Then you'd better wake her up, then, hadn't you? We're searching for a wanted man. A froggie *parlez-vous*. As big a smuggling rogue as anyone in Chacehampton—naming no names. We want him. Your Miss Somerford's beauty sleep don't count, Mister Haines. Wake her up and tell her the house has to be searched."

Haines inclined his head and left the basement. Corralie stood on the landing in her lace wrap. "I heard you say I was asleep, so I thought I had better look as if I had been. What's wrong?" She saw the look on his face.

"That sergeant insists on searching the house, Miss Corralie."

She gripped the balustrade weakly. *Oh, no—* "If my father were here, he would send them off. Could I do it, do you think?"

"You're a Somerford, Miss Corralie. Tell him to go."

"And rouse his suspicions that we do indeed have something to hide?" She sighed. "And I felt so certain they would not come here."

"Go down, Miss Corralie—and do not concern yourself about anything. I can conceal the *monsieur*." He nodded, smiling. "All will be well yet."

She stared at him and then turned, going slowly down the stairs.

Charles stood as the butler came quickly up the stairs. "What's wrong?"

"Follow me, *monsieur*—I trust only that you have a head for heights."

Charles followed him to the landing below and along toward the farthest door. Haines went into the narrow room where the maids kept the fresh linen, and then opened the tiny window that overlooked the park. "The ivy's grown strong here, *monsieur*. If you can get through the window and cling to the ivy, I think we shall fool them yet."

"Get through that mousehole?"

"Needs must when the Devil drives, *monsieur*."

"No doubt." Charles climbed up on a stool and began to wriggle through the narrow opening. "It is as well that I am renowned for my thinness."

He reached for the fluttering ivy, his fingers searching for the sturdy stems so tight against the wall, and then he eased himself from the safety of the window and put his weight on the plant. It ripped a little and he held his breath, expecting it to come away from the wall and catapult him to his death far below. But the ivy held. The wind whined around the eaves above his head and he looked up to see Haines's head outlined in the window.

"I will come as soon as I can, *monsieur*," said the butler.

"And I, *monsieur* Haines, will hold on as long as I can. I promise you."

The window closed.

Haines took a pile of towels from a shelf and put them on the window sill, and then took the stool away. He rescued the tray from the attic and took it swiftly to Corralie's room, putting it down and then turning the bed back and ruffling the crisp sheets. Then, after a final glance around, he straightened his periwig yet again and went down the stairs.

Corralie looked at the sergeant. "And why have you seen fit to have me woken up, sergeant?"

"We are still searching for the Frenchman who landed down in Webley Bay, Miss Somerford."

"He is not here, sergeant," she said coldly.

"But I must search, Miss Somerford. My orders are to search everywhere."

She glanced around as Haines came down the stairs. "Very well, sergeant, but if any damage is done to our property, then you will be in trouble. And do not take long, for I wish to return to my bed."

Haines cleared his throat. "Perhaps, sergeant, you should start from the top of the house and work down—in that way Miss Somerford may return to her sleep the sooner."

The sergeant nodded curtly at his men. "Let's get on with it, then."

Corralie folded her hands in her lap and waited. "I trust all is well, Haines."

"So do I, Miss Corralie, so do I."

It seemed that they waited for a lifetime at least, expecting every moment to hear a shout from the floors above. But the minutes passed and all they heard were the heavy steps of the soldiers' boots and the opening and closing of doors.

Then it was over. The sergeant and his men came down the stairs empty-handed. "We found no one, Miss Somerford."

"I did not imagine for one moment that you would, sergeant," she said, getting to her feet. "Have you finished?"

"Yes, Miss Somerford," he replied uncomfortably. "My apologies——"

"Good night to you, sergeant." She swept past him and up the stairs.

Charles sat weakly on the stool in the store room, his face ashen. He smiled faintly at Haines. "*Monsieur*," he murmured, "heights in the daytime are bad enough, but at night——"

Lady Agnes gave her mantle to Haines and smiled at Reynold. "An excellent celebration, don't you think?"

He turned to the butler. "Where is my daughter?"

"Here I am, Father, what's wrong?" Corralie came down the stairs.

Reynold looked uncomfortably at Lady Agnes. "Forgive me, my dear, but something must be said. Corry—where is he, then?"

"Who?"

"Vaughan."

Lady Agnes stared at him. "Madoc? He is here?"

"No, he isn't, Lady Agnes." Corralie paused at the foot of the stairs. "And I am ashamed that you should think he was, Father."

"His blasted horse is in our stables!"

Corralie's lips parted. What could she say? "I——"

"Well, girl? Do you deny that it is his horse?"

"No."

"But he is not here?" Reynold almost shook with fury. "Are you no better than a common harlot?"

"Reynold!" Agnes put her hand on his arm. "Please, don't say things like that, not even in anger."

"Agnes, that damned nephew of yours has been making sheep eyes at my daughter, and all the while he has also been messing around with other men's women! He's to stay away from here, d'you understand me?"

Agnes took her hand away and raised her chin coldly. "Oh, *Reynold,* how could you be so superior?"

He stared at her and then at the silent Corralie. "Get to your room, girl. Immediately!"

Without a word she turned and went up the stairs.

29

Madoc went to take the bridle of the horse as Lawrence's cabriolet drew up in the courtyard. "All went well, Kendal?"

"Yes, our mutual acquaintance is safely back in his floating nest."

"And the *Janus?*"

"Put into Portsmouth. She sustained some damage when she turned so sharply in the bay here—dragged her stern on some submerged rock. Anyway, she was no match for the *Belle Marie,* which in turn was no match for the *Fair Maid.*" Lawrence smiled at Averil, who sat beside her. "We'll have the Bostoner, I fancy, eh?"

She linked her arm through his and nodded. Her eyes met Madoc's for a moment and then she smiled. She felt nothing when she saw him now. It was as if it had never been, as if there had always only been Lawrence.

Lawrence climbed down. "Everything is all right here still?"

"We have heard nothing more."

"Where is he?"

"Somerford Place."

Lawrence raised his eyebrows. "I'll warrant Reynold knows nothing of it."

"Too true, my friend."

"Well, will you tell me who the mysterious stranger is? Or must I be left wondering?"

"He is my brother-in-law. Catti's husband, Charles Beauchamp."

"A Frenchman?"

"Yes."

"I was under the impression that we were at peace with France, so why the need for the surreptitious comings and goings?"

"Charles has come from Elba, Lawrence." Madoc patted the horse's neck and grinned. "He was trying to discover Bony's plans, but it all went wrong. Perhaps it was destined to fail from the outset. However, he is in England now. It remains to convince those in authority that he is not Darnier and that he is no enemy of England."

"A minor detail, eh?"

"Damn your future father-in-law."

"Why use Darnier in the first place?"

"He was the only man prepared to undertake anything on Elba—and how was I to know then that there was such animosity between the Frenchman and Harry?"

"There is no such thing as honor among thieves—even I realize that." Lawrence took his arm and steered him away from the cabriolet. "Madoc, I am not without influence. I will do what I can for your brother-in-law."

"I was hoping you would say that."

"I don't think your sister need worry any more." Lawrence halted and looked at him. "Madoc—I use your first name now, but what I am about to say should perhaps be a little less closely uttered."

"You know, don't you?" said Madoc, after studying the other's face.

"Just stay away from her from now on."

Madoc nodded slowly. "Even if I was not prepared to, Lawrence, by your own actions of late you would appear to have closed the door in my face. She is yours."

"And if I had not closed the door?"

"I love Corry, Lawrence, and only Corry. I was wrong in what I did, but the reason seemed at the time to warrant the action." Madoc looked at the other man's tense face. "Your future wife was not unfaithful to you, Lawrence—save that she kissed me and embraced me. It was you all along, really, but you treated her too gently, and for a woman like Averil, that was not the way, was it?"

Lawrence smiled unexpectedly. "No, damn you, it wasn't. Just so long as the matter is clearly understood between us."

"It is."

"Has Corry accepted you?"

"Corry has. Yes."

"Do I detect a reservation in your reply?"

"You do. I am not acceptable to her father." To prevent any further probing, Madoc began to walk back toward the cabriolet. "I must get over to Somerford Place now and see that Charles is in fact all right."

"If he was not, I rather fancy the word would be buzzing over Chacehampton by now," said Lawrence.

"You saw any soldiers this morning?"

"No. They were seen going back to Cannutbury at first light."

"I will go, then, and face the old man's music, eh?" Madoc smiled at the other.

Lawrence held out his hand. "Good luck, Madoc."

At the cabriolet, Averil leaned forward. "You are going to Corralie?"

"Yes."

"I hope it all works out for you, truly I do."

Madoc took her hand and kissed it warmly. "As I do for you, Averil."

He watched the red cabriolet spinning across the courtyard and out under the gatehouse, and then went inside the castle to find Catti.

Haines showed Madoc and Catti into the drawing room, where Lady Agnes sat with Reynold.

"Madoc! Catti!" Lady Agnes flushed a little.

Madoc glanced at Reynold. "There is no need to explain, Aunt Agnes. Where is Corralie?"

Reynold raised his head angrily. "Out."

Lady Agnes swallowed. "I am afraid, Madoc, that there was a—a *contretemps*, so to speak."

Catti could not bear the delaying any longer, for it was only about Charles that she was interested. "Aunt Agnes, where is Charles? He is well? Please, for I cannot endure this anymore."

"Charles? I don't understand——" Lady Agnes looked helplessly at her niece.

Madoc put his arms around his shaking sister. "Corry brought Charles here last night. Is he all right?"

Reynold stared. "What the devil are you talking about? Who is Charles?"

"My sister's husband."

"And Corry brought him *here?* In damnation, why?"

"To hide him from the soldiers."

"Well, he ain't here now and neither is Corry—she rode off in a temper earlier."

Lady Agnes threw him a withering look." "A justifiable temper, I might add, Reynold. In the circumstances. Ah, Haines, a tray of coffee, how admirable. Now then, Madoc and Catti, let us sit down and be sensible about this. You say that Charles came here last night?"

"Yes."

Haines cleared his throat very noisily. "Er—excuse me, my lady, but are you talking of the young French gentleman?"

Catti looked quickly at him. "Yes, oh please yes——"

"He is upstairs in one of the attic rooms, Lady Catherine. Miss Corralie and I hid him there last night."

Reynold threw his newspaper down furiously. "Damn it all, am I not master in my own house that these things happen behind my back?"

Madoc turned to look at him. "Corry was helping me. Charles took my horse and she brought him here."

"*He* had your horse?" Reynold deliberately avoided Agnes's accusing look.

"Yes. He was put ashore by a French lugger in Webley Bay last night."

"So he's the one every damned soldier at Cannutbury has been looking for?"

"No. They are all looking for Darnier, the captain of the lugger."

"Who is where? Here, as well, I suppose."

"No. He is back aboard his ship and well on his way by now. Charles is French, as you will have gathered, and under the circumstances last night it was deemed safer to try to hide him rather than risk his coming face to face with either the army or with your friend Tindling's band of merry men. One dead Frenchman might seem as good as another, might he not?"

Reynold took a long breath. "A wise precaution, perhaps. I agree."

Catti looked imploringly at Haines. "Please, take me to my husband."

Reynold nodded at the butler, who took Catti from the room, closing the door behind them.

Agnes slowly poured the coffee from the silver pot. "Reynold, about what you said last night——"

"What about?"

"About Madoc here."

"Agnes, I don't wish to discuss it!"

"I am afraid you will have no choice, Reynold, my dear. You are being most dishonest, and a decided hypocrite, are you not?"

Reynold looked uncomfortable. "Damn it, Agnes, I don't want Corry marrying—marrying——"

"Someone like Madoc? Oh *Reynold!* Now then, tell me, the reason you gave last night—is that the *only* objection you have to my nephew?"

"Yes."

"So, you do not think him an adventurer, concerned only with getting his wicked hands on your fortune?"

Madoc stared at her. "Aunt Agnes——"

"Stay out of this, Madoc. This is strictly between Reynold and myself. Well? I am awaiting your reply, Reynold."

"No, I don't think that of him."

"Then you had best take away your other objection."

"No."

"Reynold, I kept all your letters—every single indiscreet one of them—and if you persist in staying between Corralie and Madoc, then I will show them to your daughter. Page by unwise, loving page. And when she looks at the dates of those letters, she will not have too much difficulty in putting two and two together, will she?"

He said nothing.

"Reynold? Do you want your daughter to know that you and I were far more friendly than we had any right to be—while her mother was still alive? Well, do you?"

"No, damn it!"

"Then do as you should, my love. Madoc has not been even as guilty as you and I, has he? From what you say. At least no one was married."

Reynold took a long breath, staring at the fallen newspaper. Then he looked at Madoc and nodded. "Your aunt is right, I *am* a hypocrite. You seemed to be an echo of my own past, an echo that I was ashamed of. Oh, not of your Aunt Agnes, for never would I be ashamed of her in any way, far from it. But of my own actions I was ashamed. I was not admirable. Do you love my daughter?"

"Yes."

"Marry her, then—but I'll break your damned Welsh neck if you ever play her false. And believe me, I *know* the signs of a false man."

Madoc inclined his head, smiling. "You would appear to have had experience on your side in that."

"That's as may be. Just do right by Corry."

Madoc stood. "I will. Where can I find her?"

"Don't know—she flounced off on that damned horse you gave her and I haven't seen her since."

"I'll find her. Is The Beau in your stables?"

"That the name of your horse? Yes, it's there still. Oh—Madoc, your hand." Reynold held out his hand, "If you're going to be my son-in-law, I must be sure to be on good terms with you." He smiled.

Madoc took the outstretched hand. "I'll be worthy of her, I promise you." He smiled at his aunt. "Thank you," he said, gently, bending to kiss her.

Lawrence halted the cabriolet as he saw Madoc coming toward him. "I've been to Cannutbury— your brother-in-law is no longer a fugitive, Madoc.

A word in the necessary ear, soldier to soldier, as they say."

"Thank you, Lawrence, I'm indebted to you."

"Are you looking for Corry?"

"You've seen her?"

"Yes, a short while ago. Riding toward the ford by Bascombe Woods. I called her, but she didn't answer. She looked as if she'd been crying."

"I think she had."

"Everything all right now?"

"It will be. When I find her."

"Reynold changed his mind?"

"Yes."

"Find her then, Madoc."

Madoc kicked his heels and The Beau moved past the cabriolet and on toward the woods so green in the distance.

Corralie dismounted and tied Pippit to the oak tree. She looked around the secret little clearing. This was where it all started only a few weeks ago. The meadowsweet was thicker than ever now that the summer had advanced, and its perfume drugged the warm air. She closed her eyes, the salt tears pricking them. If only——

"Corry?"

She turned. She had not heard the horse crossing the ford. "Madoc?"

He smiled. "It's all right, sweetheart—everything's all right now."

"Everything?"

"Yes—we have your father's blessing."

The tears fell down her cheeks, then. "Oh Madoc, I love you so."

"Don't cry, my darling, don't cry anymore." He pulled her into his arms and kissed her, tasting the salt tears.

ABOUT THE AUTHOR

Sandra Heath was born in 1944. As the daughter of an officer in the Royal Air Force, most of her life was spent traveling around to various European posts. She has lived and worked in both Holland and Germany.

The author now resides in Gloucester, England, together with her husband and young daughter, where all her spare time is spent writing. She is especially fond of exotic felines, and at one time or another, has owned each breed of cat.

Big Bestsellers from SIGNET

☐ **FLAME OF THE SOUTH** by Constance Gluyas.
(#E8648—$2.50)

☐ **ROGUE'S MISTRESS** by Constance Gluyas.
(#E8339—$2.25)

☐ **SAVAGE EDEN** by Constance Gluyas. (#E8338—$2.25)

☐ **WOMAN OF FURY** by Constance Gluyas. (#E8075—$2.25)*

☐ **HARVEST OF DESIRE** by Rochelle Larkin.
(#E8771—$2.25)

☐ **MISTRESS OF DESIRE** by Rochelle Larkin.
(#E7964—$2.25)*

☐ **LORD OF RAVENSLEY** by Constance Heaven.
(#E8460—$2.25)†

☐ **THE FIRES OF GLENLOCHY** by Constance Heaven.
(#E7452—$1.75)†

☐ **THE PLACE OF STONES** by Constance Heaven.
(#W7046—$1.50)†

☐ **THE QUEEN & THE GYPSY** by Constance Heaven.
(#J7965—$1.95)†

☐ **GLYNDA** by Susannah Leigh. (#E8548—$2.50)*

☐ **WINTER FIRE** by Susannah Leigh. (#E8680—$2.50)

☐ **VALENTINA** by Evelyn Anthony. (#E8598—$2.25)†

☐ **ALL THE RIVERS RUN** by Nancy Cato. (#E8693—$2.95)

☐ **LUCETTA** by Elinor Jones. (#E8698—$2.25)*

* Price slightly higher in Canada
† Not available in Canada
